Prologue

The acrid stench of fear and burnt flesh tainted her expensive perfume and quickened his pulse as he put out his cigarette on her sculpted cheekbone.

Her silent scream spasmed through her and she gurgled beneath his hand on her throat, sputtering words with no sound. Her eyes pleaded, wept, their vain tilt not so pronounced as they'd been out on the terrace yesterday evening, laughing at him in the moonlight.

His gloved hand was dark against her alabaster skin. He carefully tucked the cigarette butt into his pocket. It was a lousy, disgusting habit, but tonight had called for something special. He brought both hands to her neck, squeezing a little harder, then easing his grip before closing off her airway again—teasing her, tormenting her with the false promise of freedom.

Just as she had tormented him with her promises.

No more. *He* was the one with the power over her now. *He* was the one in control of their destinies. He couldn't be hurt. He couldn't be used. He wouldn't be denied. Strength surged through him. Dominance. Superiority. His hands jerked around her throat as the anger consumed and cleansed him.

His breath came deeper, stronger as hers constricted. He straddled her chest and sat, feeling her writhe helplessly, weakly, futilely beneath him.

"You're not so high and mighty now, are you, Gretchen?" He pulled up his stocking mask,

Man
with the Muscle

Man
with the Muscle

JULIE MILLER

First published in Great Britain 2011
by Mills & Boon, an imprint of Harlequin (UK) Limited.
Large Print edition 2011
Harlequin (UK) Limited,
Eton House, 18-24 Paradise Road,
Richmond, Surrey TW9 1SR

© Julie Miller 2010

ISBN: 978 0 263 21796 4

Harlequin (UK) policy is to use papers that are natural,
renewable and recyclable products and made from
wood grown in sustainable forests. The logging
and manufacturing process conform to the legal
environmental regulations of the country of origin.

Printed and bound in Great Britain
by CPI Antony Rowe, Chippenham, Wiltshire

JULIE MILLER

attributes her passion for writing romance to all those fairy tales she read growing up, and to shyness. Encouragement from her family to write down all those feelings she couldn't express became a love for the written word. She gets continued support from her fellow members of the Prairieland Romance Writers, where she serves as the resident "grammar goddess." This award-winning author and teacher has published several paranormal romances. Inspired by the likes of Agatha Christie and Encyclopedia Brown, Ms. Miller believes the only thing better than a good mystery is a good romance.

Born and raised in Missouri, she now lives in Nebraska with her husband, son and smiling guard dog, Maxie. Write to Julie at P.O. Box 5162, Grand Island, NE 68802-5162.

wanting her to see his eyes, to know *he* was the one who'd put her in her place. "You want to rethink saying no to me?"

She nodded.

Tears and desperation and the blood on her cheek made her look vulnerable, more human than the icy beauty who'd led him on for so many months—smiling at him, sharing conversations, accepting his gifts—yet ultimately dismissing him as if he was of no more importance than a piece of furniture. For a moment, he paused to tenderly brush aside the damp golden hair that stuck to her forehead. She looked beautiful, stretched out beneath him, begging to do his bidding. This was how it could have been between them—how it should have been. He wanted to kiss her. He nearly did. But no, he wouldn't leave even that little trace of DNA. He was too smart for that.

Too smart for all of them.

Stupid bitches.

"Too late." With a snap, he crushed her windpipe. In a matter of seconds, she was dead.

When the spark faded from her eyes, it took his rage and need with him and he breathed a sigh of relief. He reached for his bag.

Precisely three minutes later, he set about the tasks of cleaning her wounds, untying her wrists and ankles and rewinding the electrical cords before returning them to their storage compartment inside the bag. He wrapped her in her pink silk robe and carried her into the adjoining room where he laid her on the bed and arranged her just so, crossing her hands over her heart in sweet repose, draping her hair over her damaged cheek, carefully removing one of her diamond earrings and closing her eyes.

"Goodbye, sweetheart."

He returned to the opulent, oversize bathroom where he'd surprised her and quickly rolled up the drop cloth he'd used and cleaned any other signs of his presence there. Finally, he stripped off the tan coveralls he wore, packing them and his gloves inside his bag. When he was certain the upstairs hallway was clear, he hurried down the back steps and locked the bag in his vehicle outside. The music from the violins, viola and cello filtered through the crisp night air and masked his footsteps as he flicked the cigarette butt into the storm drain at the curb.

Then he straightened his jacket and jogged around to join the others at the mansion's front drive, ready to be shocked and outraged when some poor unlucky soul discovered Gretchen's body.

And the message he'd tucked beneath the covers beside her.

Chapter One

"You're the saddest bunch of heroes I've ever seen." The chiding female voice cut through the buzz of lively conversations, three different television broadcasts and the chattering clacks of pool balls breaking across a table behind Alex Taylor. "You got the guy. The D.A. will put him away."

"Let's hope." Alex slid onto the green vinyl seat in front of the Shamrock's polished walnut bar and pulled some cash from the front pocket of his jeans. Not even the bright blue eyes and sympathetic smile of Josie Nichols standing on the other side could shake him from the mood he was in. "I need to order some beers."

"Hello?" The bartender slapped her washrag on top of the bar with a purpose, demanding his full attention before glancing over at the flat-screen TV hanging in the corner behind her. "You hope? KCPD's standoff with that gang-banger Demetrius Smith is all over the news. Getting him and his lieutenants off the streets just made Kansas City a hell of a lot safer. If I can walk out to my car at night and not have to worry about getting mugged or raped or caught in the cross fire between his gang and some-one else, then I'd say you got the job done. You should be celebrating. Not bringing down the mood of the bar."

"Smith's gotten out with nothing more than a slap on the wrist more than once. Evidence disappears. A witness decides not to testify." Alex closed his eyes and shook his head, seeing the gangly body of a ten-year-old boy cradled in Sergeant Delgado's arms as he crouched down behind an alley fence, waiting for their commanding officer's all-clear order. He'd have thought the kid was sleeping if it hadn't been for all the blood on Delgado's uniform. Two bullets in such a tiny body—and there'd been nothing they could do. Alex opened his eyes, sharing a bit of the grim truth that was forever etched in his memory. "Smith was laughing when we brought him out of that house. An innocent boy died today, and he was laughing. Like he wasn't even accountable for what happened. He's got connections we can only guess at. If the D.A. doesn't make the charges stick—"

"That won't happen this time," Josie insisted. "I can feel it in my bones. Smith's going to prison. That makes you heroes."

Try telling that to the mother of the boy they hadn't been able to save. If they'd cleared the house where Smith and his buddies had been holed up ten minutes sooner, Alex and his team of SWAT—Special Weapons and Tactics—officers might have been able to get him to a hospital before he bled out. Calvin Chambers didn't even have any gang tats on him. And he sure as hell hadn't fired any gun. He'd been an innocent kid cutting through the wrong backyard at the wrong time.

Alex knew more about gang life than young Calvin probably had. He'd had the remnants of the Westside Warrior tattoo he once thought meant he belonged to something important lasered off his back a decade ago, after he'd been adopted into a real family as a teen. Once he'd been Alexis Pitsaeli, street punk and foster home nightmare with no father to speak of and a mother who prized her drug addiction more than her child. Up until Gideon and Meghan Taylor had set him straight and loved him enough to make him a Taylor, too, Alex had been headed straight to prison or an untimely death.

If Alex hadn't been adopted into the Taylor

clan, it wouldn't have surprised anyone to find him shot dead in a gangbanger's backyard. But Calvin Chambers?

He swallowed the bile of irony and rage and guilt, and laid a twenty on top of the bar. "First round's on the new guy."

He nodded back to the corner table where Captain Cutler and the rest of his five-man SWAT team had taken up residence to lose the stress of the day to booze, camaraderie or the company of one of the pretty ladies who seemed to get a thrill out of flirting with the cops who frequented the Kansas City bar. Raucous laughter from the corner table bounced off the walls. Great. He'd missed the joke. It had probably been on him, anyway. Though he'd been on the force for five years now, he'd only been a member of SWAT for eight months. It was like surviving his rookie year all over again.

"Five drafts and some pretzels," he ordered.

Josie shook her dark brown ponytail down

her back and pushed the twenty dollars beneath his fingers. "You need to learn the rules of the house, Taylor. On a night like this, the first round's on me." Apparently, she was more intuitive than a cheerleader. "I'm sorry about that boy. I know it's hard to lose anyone on a call like that. But you didn't shoot him."

"I didn't get him home safe to his mom, either."

A bit of temper flared in the bartender's cheeks. "Smith and his thugs are the only ones you should be blaming. You and Rafe, Trip, Holden and the captain ought to all be commended for stopping those losers. That drug house was just outside a school zone. Kids walk by there every day. Bringing guns and drugs and violence into a family neighborhood just… galls me. As far as I'm concerned, we're lucky no one else died. And we owe that to you and your team."

Josie shivered from the top of her head to

the hem of her jeans as the emotions worked through her system, and Alex felt his lips curve with half a smile. "So how do you really feel about it?"

She reached across the bar and flicked his shoulder with the towel. "Don't you get smart with me, Taylor." Rocking back on her heels, she pointed a big-sisterly finger at him. "And stop battin' those baby browns at me. I can't help it when I get my Irish up."

"Yes, ma'am." Somehow, she'd successfully broken through the gloom and doom that had settled around his shoulders. Yes, a boy had died tragically today. But many more would be safe because of his SWAT team's actions. For the sake of Josie's smile, he'd look on the bright side.

"There'll be no *ma'am*ing around here, hot-shot. Heck, I bet I'm younger than you. What are you, twenty-six?"

"Twenty-seven."

"Ha." She tapped her thumb against her chest. "Twenty-four. So no *ma'am*s. And put your money away—it's no good here."

When she turned around to pull out five frosted glasses and start drawing beers, Alex stuffed the twenty into her tip jar. He didn't know Josie all that well, beyond the fact she was a slain cop's daughter and could play a mean game of pool. But he'd seen the thick backpack and textbooks that meant she was in school, and suspected that tending bar at the Shamrock was how she supported herself. He wasn't going to let her big heart and true blue loyalty to KCPD keep her from putting food on the table.

While he waited for her to set up the tray of drinks and pour a bowlful of pretzels, Alex let his gaze wander back to the news broadcast on the television. Michael Cutler, the leader of SWAT Team One and the man who'd recruited Alex from a list of prospective beat cop candidates to join KCPD's most highly trained and specialized response team, was finishing up a recorded interview with the reporter. Cutler's tall build and salt-and-pepper hair cut a commanding figure as he answered the blonde woman's questions. Cutler was a good ace—he reminded Alex a lot of his own adoptive father, Gideon Taylor, the fire department's chief arson investigator. He was no-nonsense, tough, but fair.

Cutler handled the interview with the same confident air of calm with which he ran the unit, explaining their mission to assist the drug task force in storming the house while protecting the security of the officers on the scene. When the reporter asked whether he thought the cops or someone in Smith's gang had shot that boy, a pointed glare from Cutler indicated the interview was over.

With the reporter on live back in the studio, Alex watched the tape continuing in the corner of the screen, showing Trip and Sergeant Delgado escorting a handcuffed Demetrius Smith into the back of a police car while Captain Cutler and Holden Kincaid stood guard over Smith's two compatriots being loaded into another black-and-white. Alex was nowhere to be seen in the camera shot. He'd had the inglorious duty of stowing gear and coordinating cleanup with the task force.

A gofer with a gun and body armor. Despite eight months of training and working together, he was still definitely the new guy. Any friendship, respect or trust Delgado, Kincaid and Trip showed him was on a strictly trial basis. He had yet to earn anything more permanent.

As the reporter turned to do a live interview in the studio with Kansas City's D.A., Dwight Powers, Alex's thoughts wandered. He half suspected that the main reason he'd gotten the SWAT position over several other older, more tenured candidates was because he was a Taylor. In addition to his dad's work in conjunction with the police department, his uncle Mitch was chief of the Fourth Precinct. His uncle Mac ran the day shift at the crime lab. He had two other uncles who were cops, and one who was an FBI agent assigned to the Kansas City Bureau. His uncle Brett, the only one who wasn't involved in law enforcement, was married to a cop.

His adopted brother, Edison Pike Taylor, worked in the K-9 unit. His two youngest brothers, Matthew and Mark, while still in college, were both already on their way to similar careers.

With a powerful, venerated family history like that, it made good press within the department to assign one of the next generation of Taylor cops to KCPD's premiere SWAT unit. But it didn't mean a thing to the members of his team.

Especially when a cop had to die for the position to open up in the first place.

Not only was Alex the new guy, he had the unenviable task of replacing a well-loved friend who'd been shot down in the line of duty. He had a lot to prove no matter how he looked at it.

Better content himself with fetching the beer.

The wry thought faded when another photo popped up on the TV screen beside Smith's booking picture. The woman looked delicate, pretty in an icy-hot way. Striking light red hair. Creamy skin. Wide, slightly full, could-be-sexy-if-they-weren't-pressed-so-tight lips. She was a stunning contrast to Smith's mahogany skin and shaved head. She was all class, all uptown, compared to Smith's decidedly downtown street style.

Beauty aside, noting her knowing arch of one auburn brow, Alex could tell there was some fire under that buttoned-up suit and cool facade, as well. He'd bet those lips softened like honey when she smiled. He wondered what it would take to get her to smile, what a man might do to ignite the fire beneath the surface of her skin.

Alex's pulse shook off the last of its doldrums

and beat at a healthy tempo. Nothing like a little sensual delight to take a man's mind off his troubles. He tuned into the story—something about the attorney taking on Smith's prosecution—trying to catch the name of the flame-haired fantasy.

Audrey Kline. Audrey. He grinned at how well the old-fashioned name fit her tailored suit and pearls. Was she another reporter covering the story? She must be new to this station since he hadn't seen…

Wait a minute. *Assistant District Attorney* Audrey Kline?

Alex's pulse tripped over a warning as recognition kicked in. He leaned in slightly, tuning out the noise of the bar around him and reading the words scrolling across the bottom of the screen.

Audrey Kline—daughter of Rupert Kline of Kline, Galloway & Tucker, Attorneys at Law. *That* name he recognized. Rupert Kline was one of the—if not *the*—most revered lawyers in Kansas City. His firm often represented the wealthiest of clients and, more than once, had poked holes in the tightest of KCPD's cases and gotten various slime bags freed or released from jail time with little more than a slap on the wrists.

The enemy was arguing Smith's case?

"No way." Alex's Latin blood hummed through his veins as irritation mixed with the initial attraction he'd felt.

What the hell was the D.A. thinking, putting a pampered society princess in charge of prosecuting Demetrius Smith? Did he really think some rookie wannabe was equipped to handle one of Kansas City's most important cases? Nailing Smith for any number of charges, from drug trafficking and assault to witness intimidation and murder, would put a substantial dent in the city's gang activities and violent crime stats.

He hadn't risked his life to bring Smith in—

Calvin Chambers hadn't died—so that Red there could play at her daddy's game and get her picture on TV. Audrey Kline was too young, too pretty, too…fluffy…to be taken seriously and win the case.

What was she doing working for the city when she could be handling contracts or civil suits at Daddy's law firm, anyway? Was there some kind of political agenda going on here? If that murdering SOB Smith got off because Dwight Powers wanted to do a favor for her father…

"You okay, Taylor?" Josie was demanding his attention again.

Alex checked his temper as well as his hormones as the bartender scooted a bowl of pretzels across the bar. "Yeah. Just caught up in the news of the day, I guess."

"I can change the channel," she offered.

He shook his head and stood, tamping down the frissons of unexpected frustration and desire still sparking through his system. "I'm good. I'd better get back to the party."

"If you take this to the table, I'll bring the drinks over in just a sec." She pointed to the waitress standing at the end of the bar. "I need to get her order filled first."

"Sure."

Audrey Kline's picture disappeared and Alex cursed himself for breathing easier. *Stupid move, Taylor.* Twisting his shorts into a knot over some woman he'd never even met and a case that was out of his hands.

He tucked his money clip back into the pocket beneath his badge. Must be the guilt of the day combined with the pressure of the past year that left him feeling the need to connect to the right woman and get some of this pent-up frustration out of his system. He wasn't getting anything but a friendly one-of-the-guys vibe from Josie, and he was cool with that.

But Audrey Kline? One head shot on the news

and he'd been thinking of ways he could peel those pinstripes off her. So maybe he'd been a little obsessed with work lately, and hadn't really dated since he'd accepted the SWAT gig. Needs that had been put on hold for too long, simmering too close to the surface, were the only reasons that made sense when it came to explaining his instant awareness of the red-haired attorney and his knee-jerk reaction to her assignment to the Smith case.

Logic said there could never be anything but distance between a rich daddy's girl like her and a streetwise cop like him. She probably owned shoes that cost more than his monthly salary. Unless she went slumming for some secret kind of sex life, he could guarantee that a former gang member turned weapons and recon specialist for KCPD wasn't the kind of guy she'd even deign to notice—much less want to connect with.

And an attorney who lacked the *cojones* to go

after Smith and win wasn't the kind of woman *he* wanted to be with anyway, right?

Carrying the oversize pretzel bowl in one hand, Alex made his way between a row of booths and two pool tables, sparing a moment to trade winks with a cool blonde. *That* was who he should be gettin' the hots for. She was interested, willing—and not responsible for bringing Demetrius Smith to justice. But he moved on with a thanks-but-no-thanks smile when giggles and chatter erupted around her table. Too perky. Too easy. While Alex wasn't averse to spending time with a beautiful woman, he just wasn't in the mood for light and playful and meaningless tonight.

Besides, he had a feeling that if he didn't deliver these snacks soon, he'd drop even further down that invisible hierarchy of prove-you-deserve-to-be-here attitude he got from the members of his team.

"Pretzels are up," Alex announced, setting the

bowl on the table and sliding it to the middle. "Josie's bringing the drinks."

"Thanks, shrimp." Joseph Jones, Jr., nick-named Triple J and often shortened to Trip, stuck a finger into the thick paperback book he was reading and helped himself to a handful of the salty twists.

So Alex was only five-ten. He hated the nick-name Trip had stuck him with. Of course, as tall and powerfully built as the tank-size Trip was, anyone under six feet probably seemed small. "At least my mama knew more than one letter of the alphabet when she was coming up with names."

Trip looked up from his book as the others, in-cluding Holden Kincaid on his cell phone beside him, laughed. "Good one, peewee."

Yeah. Like that was better than *shrimp.*

"Thank Josie." Alex pulled out a chair and took a seat between Sergeant Delgado and

Captain Cutler. "She saw us on the news. She wouldn't take my money."

"What? Hell." Rafe Delgado glanced over his shoulder at the bar where Josie and her uncle, the Shamrock's owner, Robbie Nichols, were busy serving drinks. "She can't afford that."

"I left a twenty in the tip jar for her," Alex assured him.

"Can't even get one lousy order straight," he grumbled. The lanky, dark-haired sergeant spun his chair around and shoved it under the table. "I'm going to see if I can at least save her the trip over here."

"She's the one who offered to—"

But Rafe was already striding away. Alex turned at the strong hand that squeezed his shoulder. Captain Cutler's typically stoic expression was eased by a fatherly smile. "Let him go, son. It's not personal."

The reprimand sure felt as if he'd insulted

Josie in some way. And he hadn't meant to. "I paid her for the drinks, I swear."

"I know you did. And somewhere under the strain of having that boy die in his arms this afternoon, he knows it, too." Cutler swatted Alex's shoulder and pulled away, including the other two men at the table with them in his explanation for the sergeant's abrupt departure. "Josie's a hell of a lot prettier to look at than any of you. With what we've been through today, I don't blame Rafe for choosing her company over your ugly mugs."

"Sarge likes her?" Alex asked.

"I think it's more of an overprotective big brother thing," Cutler explained. "His first partner when he joined KCPD out of the academy was her dad. He's watched her grow up."

"So no hitting on Josie or Delgado will cut you off at the knees, shrimp." In one smooth motion, Trip pointed a warning finger at Alex and scooped up half the pretzels remaining in the bowl. He glanced over the top of his book. "And you can't afford to be any shorter."

Alex flicked a pretzel across the table, hitting Trip in the middle of his forehead. The book went down on the table. Alex caught the pretzel that came flying back at him and crushed it in his fist, crumbling the dregs down into the bowl.

"Oh, you da man, Taylor."

"That's right, big guy. I'm the man."

"Children..." Captain Cutler warned with a smirk of his own.

Alex's and Trip's respective pretzels were dutifully stuffed into their own mouths. The silliness of the interchange lightened Alex's mood, and while Trip went back to reading with a grin, Alex turned to spot Sergeant Delgado plucking the tray of beers from Josie's hands and trying to squeeze a word in through the argument his actions triggered.

They were finally shaking off the grim events

of the day. SWAT Team One was going to be okay. Alex was fitting in. No one was on his case for being too new, too young, too short—too lucky to have this job because he was a Taylor—too anything. He shifted his shoulders inside the black cotton sweater and leather jacket he wore and relaxed against his chair.

"Liza said to tell everyone hi." Sharpshooter Holden ended the call to his wife and set his cell phone on the table. "I'm leaving after the first drink. I have orders to come home with cookie dough ice cream or not to show up at all." He tapped his cell phone and grinned in a boyishly excited way that belied his ability to go stone-cold still to make a kill shot or bring down a suspect. "With the way her appetite's kicking into high gear, I think we could be having the baby any day now."

Captain Cutler chewed around a pretzel as he spoke. "I thought Liza wasn't due until Christmas."

"It's practically Thanksgiving already."

"In two weeks. You're hopeless, Kincaid."

"Oh, and when you and Jillian decide to start making babies, you're going to be all cool, calm and collected about it?" Holden challenged with a grin.

The captain smoothed his palm across the top of his short, salt-and-pepper hair. "I have a teenage son. I know about making babies."

"So you and Jillian *are* working on giving Mikey a little brother?"

"Mind your own business, Kincaid."

"Or maybe a little sister." Holden whistled through his teeth. "I'd hate to be the guy who tried to date her."

Alex easily pictured an image of Captain Michael Cutler, suited up in body armor, weapons and badge, greeting an already-nervous teenage boy at the front door. His daughter's unsuspecting date would probably pee his pants. Wisely, Alex buried his amusement by pulling the snacks away from Trip and helping himself to a bite before they were all gone. Only golden-boy Holden could get away with such teasing.

"You finished?" The captain arched an eyebrow as Holden's chuckle erupted into laughter.

"I can't hear myself think over here," Trip groused, giving Alex the evil eye as he easily reached across the table and pulled the pretzels back in front of him.

"You can think?" Holden snatched the book and the bowl from his hands before pointing to the booths behind Alex. "Read on your own time. Single women. Go."

Trip grabbed the book right back, but turned his focus to Cutler. "Permission to take him down, sir?"

The captain grimaced, looking very much like a babysitter who'd lost control of his charges. "Where are those beers?"

"Right here." Rafe Delgado had returned, seemingly even more grumpy than when he had left. He plopped the tray down, sending foam cascading over the top of the frosty pilsner glasses. "Help yourselves."

Wisely, each man kept his comments about the testy waiter to himself and reached for a beer.

Holden's phone vibrated on the tabletop just as the cell on Alex's belt buzzed. He set down his beer and wiped his hand on the leg of his jeans before answering. Trip and Sarge were opening their phones, too, as Captain Cutler's went off. The noise of the bar instantly muted and the tension around the table thickened as the captain picked up the call. Alex checked his watch. After 10:00 p.m. They'd been off the clock for more than an hour. A call summoning KCPD's premiere SWAT team at this time of night couldn't be good.

Alex was clearing the *Call Dispatch* message off his touch screen when the captain rejoined them at the table. "Got it. My men are still with me—I'll notify them. Cutler out." He disconnected the call and addressed the team. "Hold off on those drinks." He glanced at Holden. "Tell Liza the ice cream will have to wait."

"What's up, boss?" Alex asked.

"Looks like we're getting some overtime to-night. Rafe, I need you to head on back to HQ to get the van. We'll need all our equipment. We'll meet you at the Plaza address Dispatch gave and suit up there."

"Yes, sir." Rafe nodded, his surly mood hidden behind a face that was pure business. He grabbed his jacket and jogged out the door.

"Captain?" Holden prompted. They still didn't have an explanation for the off-duty call.

"Looks like we've got another Rich Girl murder. Banking family this time. The Cos-grove estate. They found Cosgrove's daughter strangled to death in her bedroom. Signs of tor-ture." Cutler muttered a curse under his breath. "There was a party going on downstairs when they found her. Almost a hundred people on the scene with a dead woman upstairs."

"That's ballsy." Holden voiced what Alex was thinking. "Sounds as though this guy is trying to flaunt his crime."

"That's the second death with that kind of victim in just over a year, isn't it?" Trip asked, sliding a bookmark between the pages of his paperback and cramming it into the pocket of his jacket. "The first one's never been solved. I thought a task force had been set up to narrow down a suspect."

"Yeah." Alex frowned. They were men of action. Troubleshooters. Protectors. They weren't the cops who sifted through clues at crime scenes. "Why call us instead of homicide?"

"It's up to us to secure the scene so the detectives and CSI can get in and do their job."

"We're on crowd control?"

"Not exactly." The captain pulled his

KCPD SWAT jacket from the back of his chair and shrugged into it. "The perp's upping his game. The party's no coincidence. This time he left a bomb threat with the body."

Chapter Two

Audrey Kline squinted against the swirling strobe effect of the four police cars and other official vehicles lined up on the street in front of the Cosgrove mansion as she climbed out of her Mercedes and tried to make sense of what was going on here. The scene outside the sprawling stone house resembled the aftermath of some kind of natural disaster, with people huddling under blankets, women wearing their escorts' suit jackets over designer dresses, one man sitting at the back of an ambulance with a blood pressure cuff around his arm, and many others silently weeping.

It was true. It hadn't been some cruel tabloid rumor that had blipped past on her local internet news site.

Gretchen was dead.

The certainty of it hit her like a punch to the gut and, for a moment, she sagged against the open door, her shocked breaths forming frosty clouds in the damp November air. How? Why?

Screeching brakes alerted her a split second before the glare of headlights spun around the corner half a block away, hitting her square in the face. A television news van. Audrey turned away and closed the car door, instinctively shielding her face from the unwelcome intrusion.

There was already a slew of other reporters here, searching for someone noteworthy from the wealthiest and most powerful of Kansas City society to give them a sound bite. And more of those underground bloggers who'd broken the news of the murder half an hour ago were probably mingling with the guests, texting away.

But Audrey was in no mood to be a media darling tonight. Gretchen's death was personal. Private. She needed answers. She needed this to make sense. This was the second friend she'd lost in the past two years. Her mother had died the year before that. Standing around and waiting with the others would only give her time to feel, to remember, to hurt. And to have that kind of weakness caught on tape and posted in the public eye would only make the grief that much tougher to deal with. If she ever wanted to be known as something more than Rupert Kline's little princess, then weakness wasn't something anyone here was going to get a chance to observe.

With newfound resolve giving her strength, Audrey buttoned up the front of her cashmere blazer, stuffed her keys into the pocket of her jeans and slipped through the suits and cocktail dresses of the party guests gathered outside the front gate. They parted like zombies, shocked and murmuring, as she made a beeline for the uniformed policeman standing by the driveway's wrought-iron gates. "Excuse me, officer? I'm a friend of the family."

Her father had taught her that standing as tall as her five feet five inches allowed and walking and talking with a purpose usually convinced people that she belonged wherever she wanted to be. But the young officer wasn't fooled. Leaving one arm resting on his belt beside his gun, he raised his hand to stop her. "I'm sorry, miss. No one's allowed to come inside the gate."

She tilted her chin to argue that she belonged here. "My father and Mr. Cosgrove went to Harvard together. I don't think he would mind…"

And then she saw the two detectives—one tall and light-haired, jotting notes, the other shorter and darker— talking to a pair of crime scene investigators, each wearing their reflective vests and holding their bulky kits in their hands. What were they doing outside the house? Had something happened on the grounds, as well? The blip she'd seen on her laptop said the victim had been found in her bedroom upstairs.

Why weren't they interviewing suspects? Taking pictures? Why were they just standing around? Didn't they know what a beautiful soul Gretchen had been? How much her parents and friends had loved her? Why weren't they tearing that house apart to find out who'd killed her?

Audrey took a deep breath to cool her frustration, wishing she'd taken the time to don a suit and high heels instead of quickly pulling on jeans and a jacket over her pajamas. She'd been up late working at home instead of attending Gretchen's party where she might have been able to do some good by kick-starting the investigation and putting these people to work. With no makeup and her hair hanging down to her shoulders in loose waves, she knew she looked more like a teenager than a grown woman. But she wasn't about to let her appearance stop her anymore than had the two red lights she'd run speeding across town to get here.

She'd known Gretchen Cosgrove since kindergarten. Their adult paths had taken them in different directions, but they saw each other at social functions like this one often enough to keep in touch. A friendship like that didn't die. A woman Audrey's own age shouldn't die.

"Please." She reached into her back pocket and looped the lanyard with her Office of the District Attorney identification badge around her neck. The job was new, her switch from private practice to public prosecutor a calculated bid to establish her independence beyond the shadow cast by her father. She hadn't had the opportunity to pull rank without her father's influence to back her up yet. But this was as good a time to try as any. "I'm an officer of the court. I'm sure there's something I can do to help."

"Sorry, ma'am," the officer apologized, "but my orders are strict. Nobody crosses the cordon tape until SWAT clears the scene, not even the commissioner herself."

"I don't understand. Wasn't the body found a couple hours ago? The crime scene is getting cold."

His gaze dropped down to her ID badge. Apparently, the judicial emblem held enough sway for him to lean in to whisper. "There may be a bomb inside."

"A bomb?"

He put a finger to his lips. "That's what the note with the body said. Captain Cutler said until we know more, we don't want to say or do anything that will cause a panic."

Cutler. She knew that name. That meant his SWAT team was on the premises, and that Gretchen's death might not be the only tragedy KCPD had to worry about. Audrey glanced around, recognizing many of the guests in attendance. There was the party planner Audrey had hired herself in the past, Clarice Darnell, along with her staff—servers, caterers, parking attendants. These were friends, colleagues, acquaintances Audrey had met at society events similar to this one. They were already traumatized by the news that their hostess tonight had been murdered. She didn't wish more trouble on any of them. "No. We wouldn't."

"You can check with me later," the policeman offered. "I'll let you in as soon as Captain Cutler gives the okay."

She nodded her thanks. "In the meantime, is there someone in charge I could speak with to get some details about what's happened? It's already on the internet. Rumors are going to fly if we don't contain this."

"Ma'am, all I've been told is to keep people back—"

"Never mind." She put up her hands, knowing she was pushing too hard, knowing he was just doing his job, knowing she wouldn't get her answers here. "Thank you."

"Audrey?"

She turned at the familiar voice and hurried to meet the tall blond man striding toward her. "Harper."

He wrapped his arms around her waist and lifted her clear off the ground, squeezing her tight as he wept against her neck. "She's gone, Audrey. Gretchen's gone." She held on tight and rocked back and forth with him. "I loved her, you know."

"I know. We all did."

He gulped in a shuddering breath and eased his grip enough so her toes could touch the ground. "We were always together at school—you, me, Gretchen, Charlotte, Donny, Val and the others."

Audrey rubbed circles at the collar of his

gabardine suit, inhaling his familiar scents of tobacco and aftershave, sharing the loss with him. Their whole group of friends through high school had been tight, and though their lives and jobs had taken them in different directions after graduation, they'd found a way to keep in touch, trading calls and notes, coming together in times of tragedy like tonight.

"I used to think you were the one." Harper sighed, recalling the brief time they'd dated in high school. "But when I got back from law school, something about Gretch had changed. She was still as beautiful and fun and goofy as ever, but…"

"She grew up." She'd seen the new maturity in the once-capricious Gretchen, too.

"I asked her to marry me. We were going to announce it tonight."

That she didn't know. Tears welled up in Audrey's eyes, and she pulled back to touch his face. "Oh, Harper."

"I saw her tonight. In her bed. Before the cops chased us out." His red-rimmed eyes were dry now, and a brave smile creased his face. "You know she never gets anywhere on time—she changes her mind about what she's wearing or can't find the right jewelry to match. But after the guests had been here for almost an hour, I got worried. I went upstairs to…" His smile faltered and Audrey's stomach clenched to receive the blow. "She looked so perfect lying there, like she was sleeping. But she… That bastard hurt her. Tortured her. There were marks around her wrists and neck. Her face was… I touched her and she…she was so cold."

Audrey looped her arms around his neck and hugged him again, hiding her own face against the starch of his collar. "I'm so sorry."

"It's just like Val all over again." They'd consoled each other the night Valeska Gordeeva Gallagher had been murdered, too. "Only, I never saw Val's body until the visitation at the funeral home. I saw Gretch—"

"Shh, Harp. Don't think of that. Let's remember how beautiful Gretchen and Val were."

"You're right. You're always right. I can count on you to say the right thing, can't I?" Someone jostled them in the crowd and Harper pulled away, straightening his tie, breathing deeply, tightening his jaw to keep the tears from falling again. "She's not coming back. I'll never see her smile or hear her laugh again."

With that grim pronouncement, the first tears spilled over onto Audrey's cheeks. She quickly swiped them away. "Harper—"

"I'd better get back to her parents. The press want them to say something. I've been running interference." He bent down to press a chaste kiss to her forehead. "They'll be glad to know you're here."

Another tear burned in the corner of her eye. She sniffed as her sinuses began to congest.

Harper might have sucked it up, but she needed a minute to compose herself. "I'll be over to talk to them soon."

"Gotta go."

He walked away, leaving her shaking. She'd listened and offered comfort without realizing how much she needed it herself. They might not have been the closest of friends anymore, or else she would have known about the engagement— Gretchen had chosen a social path while Audrey had focused on her career—but she had been her oldest friend. And now there was a spot inside her, splitting open, emptying out, leaving grief and regret and helplessness in its place.

Audrey pressed a fist to her trembling lips and surveyed the crowd. She wasn't going to lose it here. The size of the gathering had nearly doubled with press and police, people who knew the Cosgroves and curious strangers. She couldn't expect to hold on to her anonymity much longer, yet she couldn't afford to be spotted as a bawling wreck—not if she wanted to impress her father and his old-school cronies, not if she intended to win the case she'd been assigned this afternoon and solidify her position in the D.A.'s office.

But the tears were burning for release. Hugging her arms in front of her, Audrey ducked her head and shuffled through the crowd, trying to draw as little attention as possible as she desperately sought out a private refuge. Her exposed skin would flush with every emotion she was feeling—a telltale, redheaded curse she'd endured her whole life—and there'd be no hiding the ache blooming inside her.

She shifted directions, deciding she should just get inside her car and drive away. But she stopped when she reached the curb. A camera crew was setting up a remote broadcast post on the opposite side of the street, and they'd recognize her as soon as she walked by.

Her throat raw from the constriction of emotions she held in check, Audrey turned and followed the sidewalk around the fringe of the gathering and just kept walking. Once she realized the voices from the crowd were fading, she stopped and raised her head, pulling her hair back from her face and tucking it behind her ears. She'd nearly reached the neighbor's house an eighth of a mile away.

There was her sanctuary. Not the house, but the red-leafed hedgerows and iron fencing that ran between the two properties. With the press and police focused at the front of the estate, the side yards were empty, shadowed and blessedly quiet. Audrey glanced behind her to Gretchen's house. They'd played hide-and-seek together on the massive grounds when they were children, and the memories of Gretchen's easy laugh and adventurous imagination reignited the grief that was set to consume her.

She needed to get out of here. Now.

She darted around the brick pillar at the corner of the Cosgroves' fence. *Oh, Lord.*

The security lights in the neighbor's front yard flashed on, reflecting off the white gold of her watch band. Reacting like the trespasser she was, Audrey tugged the sleeve of her jacket over her wrist and crouched down between the fence and hedge. The night was conspiring against her efforts to find a private moment to acknowledge her grief and center herself. Maybe she should just curl up in a ball here and let the tears flow.

But that would only add fuel to the paparazzi's rumor mill if they discovered an assistant district attorney huddled in the mud behind a burning bush shrub outside a crime scene.

"Why didn't I just stay home?" she muttered. Yet, as her jeans soaked up the chilly dampness from the ground beneath her knee, Audrey saw that she hadn't triggered the security lights, after all.

Instead, she got a clear look at the culprit. An

armed SWAT cop, wearing a flak vest over his black uniform, was lugging a large metal box to the back of the SWAT van parked in the driveway. Where had he come from? He was grinching to himself, maybe complaining about setting off the lights with his approach.

He set the box on the van's bumper with a heavy thunk, and the entire vehicle rocked, giving an indication as to the considerable weight he'd carried. The man unsnapped the strap beneath his chin and pulled off his helmet, dropping it to the concrete at his feet before scrubbing his black-gloved fingers over the top of his hair.

For a moment, Audrey forgot about the reporters and the mud and her grief. As he opened the back doors and hefted the box inside, his movements caught the lights in his short dark hair, revealing blue-black glints in the rumpled waves. Was he packing up? Did that mean the house had been cleared? The bomb discovered and dismantled?

He had the doors closed before she could think to move, and now she was forced to kneel there until the motion-detector lights went back off or the officer climbed inside the van. But he didn't appear to be in any hurry. With his rifle looped casually through the crook of his arm, he slowly turned, taking note of the vehicles in the street, the neighbors scurrying along the sidewalk to get a closer look at all the activity. Apparently oblivious to the approach of winter in the air, he unbuttoned the cuffs of his black shirt and rolled up the sleeves over a pair of muscular forearms. With a simple tilt of his head, he spoke into the microphone strapped to his Kevlar vest.

He was on guard, looking for something or someone, scanning his surroundings, his dark gaze skimming past her hiding spot. Audrey hugged her arms closer to her body and made herself even smaller. Had he seen her? Sensed her presence? She could hide from friends and avoid the press, but something about the intensity of those watchful eyes warned her that it would be very hard to keep anything hidden from him.

Audrey held her breath. Waited. Tried to ignore the little tingles of awareness sparking beneath the emotions she held so tightly in check. He wasn't as tall as Harper or even her father. But he was all muscle, all alertness, all coiled energy. If the killer had planted a bomb inside the Cosgrove house, he looked like the type of man who could take care of it. He looked like the type of man who could have saved Gretchen's life in the first place.

Gretchen would have called him hot. She would have been introducing herself, flirting with him by now. She would have welcomed him as a friend and made him feel glad to be a part of her life long before Audrey even decided to admit he was handsome in an earthy, unpolished sort of way.

A tear leaked out, its hot moisture chapping her cheek in the cool breeze. Gretchen would have thought hiding in the shrubs to avoid the press and spy on hot guys was a grand adventure, but for Audrey this was pure torture. Another tear trailed along the same path, marking her skin. Grief could no longer wait for privacy and a sob squeezed through her throat in a muffled gasp.

Not here. Not now. The SWAT cop's gaze swung back around and she shoved her knuckles against her lips, stifling the breathy whimper of each sob while the tears streamed over her hand. She could read the headlines now— *Lawyer Can't Handle Crime Scene, Muddy Misstep for Kline's Daughter* or *Newest A.D.A. Runs and Hides.* Just the kind of decorum and control that would inspire public confidence as she led the prosecution against gang-leader Demetrius Smith. Not.

But then a KCPD pickup pulled into the driveway behind the SWAT van and she had her chance to escape public scrutiny.

Audrey pushed to her feet, stumbling back against the iron fence, as that all-seeing cop walked up to meet the truck. Another uniformed officer—minus the armored vest and extra gear and weaponry of the first man—climbed out of the truck with a German shepherd bounding down behind him, to shake hands and trade greetings. By the time the SWAT cop had stooped down to wrestle the dog around its ears, Audrey was moving. Holding up her hand to shield her face from the prickly branches of the hedgerow, she jogged several yards along the fence until the bustle and bright lights from the front of the house could no longer be seen or heard.

She inhaled a lungful of the cool night air and

exhaled on sobs that shook through her. Curling her fingers around the cold, unyielding iron of a fence post, she held on and let the grief overtake her.

Seconds passed, maybe a minute or two, as the pain knifed through her. With one hand braced on her knee and the other gripping the fence to keep from toppling over, she wept for Gretchen and for the void her death created in so many lives, including her own. She'd never learned Gretchen's gifts for spontaneity and handling stress and sharing joy, and now she never would. Kansas City had lost a generous and enthusiastic young benefactor. Harper Pierce had lost a fiancée. The Cosgroves had lost a daughter. Audrey had lost another friend.

Finally, the sobs became little gasps and hiccups as the worst of it passed. Audrey's diaphragm ached, her sinuses throbbed against her skull, her eyes felt puffy and hot. But she could think again. She could feel something beyond the pain—anger, perhaps, determination to honor Gretchen's memory and vindicate her murder.

And she could hear.

Footsteps.

Audrey snapped her attention to the soft, even rhythm of someone moving through the Cosgroves' backyard. Although muffled by the fallen leaves and dewy grass, there was no mistaking the tread of company cutting between the garden paths and towering oaks that shaded the yard on the other side of the fence.

The police officers she'd seen all carried flashlights. But this, this was something different. A noise in the dark. The whisper of stealth.

Pushing her hair away from her hot, sticky cheeks, Audrey peered between the iron bars to identify the source of the sound among the trees. Too big to be a squirrel or rabbit. Too real for her to feel safe. The breeze rustled through the hedge, sending a chill dancing along her spine. If that was a cop, where was his flashlight? And if it wasn't, how had he gotten past security inside the front gates?

She pressed her face against the bars, trying to spot the movement among the trees. But the footsteps had fallen silent. With no sound to listen for and nothing to see, her other senses took over. The breeze was damp and cool against her skin, and it carried the subtlest hint of cigarette smoke into her nose. Since when did cops smoke on the job?

Audrey straightened, her breath still coming in stuttering gasps, her legs willing her to back away. She dabbed at her nose with the back of her hand and brushed the moisture on her pant leg. Had he gone? Was that scent the whisper of a shadow that had moved on? Or was he standing there, waiting, watching from the darkness?

Watching her?

A beam of light hit the side of her face, blinding her. With a startled yelp, she raised her hand to block the light and turned. "Stop it!" She pointed through the fence. "Were you...? How...?" Her pulse raced faster than her thoughts could keep up. *Run.* No. Even as the instinct shot through her, she knew she had no place to go. *Game face, Audrey. Get your Rupert Kline, killer-in-the-courtroom game face on.* With a noisy sniffle, she pulled back her shoulders and lifted her chin. "Could you get that light out of my face, please?"

She was going for confidence, strength, with that order. But her bout of crying and uncertain fear made the tone husky, revealing she was far more rattled than she cared to admit.

"Audrey Kline?"

Oh, boy. Here it comes. "I don't have any statement to make at this time."

"Okay."

Okay? In a moment of confusion, her strength deflated. "The light?"

Thankfully, the man tilted the flashlight down

to the ground. Not a reporter. Not a killer. He wasn't giving off a whiff of anything beyond leather and starch and clean, musky man. She didn't need to see his face to know from the width of his chest—and the assault rifle pointed down to the ground at his side—that she'd been discovered by the SWAT officer she'd been ogling only minutes earlier. "Better come out of there, ma'am."

He pulled back the hedge where she'd been hiding. No way had he just climbed that fence. She'd been so busy sobbing and sniffling, then spying through the trees, that she simply hadn't heard his approach from the opposite direction. She pointed over her shoulder as she stepped out. "There was someone over there. Maybe just having a smoke, maybe something else."

"And you were checking it out?" He let the hedge spring back into place and positioned himself between her and the noise she'd heard.

He pointed the beam of his flashlight into the trees on the other side of the fence.

"No, I..." Despite the warm, rich timbre of his voice, she detected the tinge of sarcasm there. "How do you know me?"

Apparently, he didn't see anything more than she had, although he did pause a moment to touch the microphone at his shoulder and ask someone called Trip to take another check through the Cosgroves' backyard. "You're with the D.A.'s office."

Audrey struggled to wedge her defenses back into place when he faced her with the abrupt pronouncement. "I'm afraid you have me at a disadvantage."

"I saw you on the news earlier tonight. Besides," he continued as he shone his flashlight on her chest, "I can read your name tag." He swung the light to the badge hanging from a chain around his own neck. "Alex Taylor. I'm with KCPD."

Her gaze darted from his black vest to the handgun strapped to his right thigh, over to the ominous-looking rifle and back up to dark eyes that were nearly black in the shadows. "I figured out you were a cop for myself." Her throat grated as she coughed to clear it. But she managed a smile as she moved around him. "Nice to meet you. Excuse me."

"You can't go that way."

She shrugged off the gloved hand on her arm and gestured out to the street. "Well, I can't go *that* way. I'll just cut through the neighbor's yard and circle around to my car."

"No."

"No?" She uttered a sound somewhere between a sob and a curse. "I know it means nothing to you, but I have a reputation to uphold in this city. I have on no makeup and I've been crying my eyes out. If you recognized me, then those reporters who track my every move certainly will."

"Do you always hide in the bushes when you're upset?"

"Do I hide...? You..." Audrey clamped her mouth shut as her temper rekindled other emotions. She tipped her chin to look him in the eye. "I'm not trespassing on your crime scene. All I need is the chance to slip away undetected so I embarrass neither my family nor the D.A. You can't stop me."

He took a single step and blocked her path. "Yes, I can."

Oh, God. He was serious.

Temper. Grief. Frustration. Humiliation. Any one of those could have busted through her tenuous control of her emotions. Being hit by all four at once released the flood gates again. Audrey's eyes stung.

"Don't do this." She swiped away the first tear, chiding her own weakness.

"You don't cry pretty, do you?"

She croaked on a sound that was half laugh,

half groan, and swiped at another tear, willing it to be her last. "Gee, thanks. Is that the best line you've got?"

"Never found the need to use lines. Here." He reached behind him and pulled a blue bandanna from his pocket. The hint of a smile eased the firm line of his mouth as he held out the cloth like a peace offering. "Was the woman inside a friend of yours?"

With an embarrassing snivel, Audrey nodded and snatched the gift from his fingers. She wiped her cheeks and nose, then pressed the soft cotton, still warm from the heat of his body, against her eyes. "Thank you."

"There's nothing pretty about losing an innocent life, is there?"

Although his hushed voice was as dark and soothing as the night around them, she got the faint impression that he was speaking about something personal rather than philosophical. Audrey shook her head. "No, there's not."

He shifted his stance, his eyes sweeping the area around them. "Look, I'm not trying to be a hard-ass when you're clearly dealing with something here. But KCPD has established a perimeter and wants to control the crowd for a reason."

"I heard about the bomb."

"We're thinking that was an empty threat—neither the dogs nor my team have found anything." He nodded his head toward the street. "But it got the perp the response he wanted. Detective Montgomery—he's in charge of the investigation—thinks the killer is getting off on all this attention. Chances are he's here somewhere, watching."

Audrey tensed and glanced over her shoulder, remembering the footsteps she'd heard.

"So you can see why it might not be too smart to wander off on your own."

She turned her gaze back to Alex Taylor's face, feeling more than a little unsettled by the possibility he was suggesting. "There has to be a hundred people involved with the party to-night. Double that if you count all the press and cops and curiosity seekers. You really think the killer is one of them?"

"I'm not the detective. But I do make sure everyone stays safe. Especially someone from the D.A.'s office who has a major trial coming up."

"What do you know about that?"

"Like I said, I watch the news. I'm one of the men who brought in Demetrius Smith. You cannot let that murderer walk."

"I'll do my best."

"I'd like it better if you said you were sure you could win. Or if D.A. Powers was handling the case himself."

Audrey bristled at the dig. It wasn't the first time someone had doubted her abilities because of her looks or her father's bank account or the fact she turned red in the face when she lost control of her emotions. "No one bought my law degree for me, Mr. Taylor. And I didn't just earn it—I was top of my class. I've worked as a defense attorney and now for the prosecution, so I know criminal law inside and out. I asked for this assignment, and Dwight Powers gave it to me because he knew I could handle it."

Did he just take an accusatory step toward her? "So you *are* trying to make a name for yourself with this trial."

Not in the glory-seeking way he was implying. Audrey tilted her chin and met the charges head-on. "I'm doing my job. I only got the case this afternoon. Just because I haven't had a chance to weigh all the options to develop a prosecution strategy yet doesn't mean I'm going to lose."

"He killed a ten-year-old boy today and didn't bat one eye of remorse. He's not going to be afraid of you."

Audrey saw the anger tighten his jaw, felt the pain radiating through the edge of his voice and regretted getting on her soapbox. It explained the "innocent life" remark he'd made earlier. Despite the sting of his doubts about her abilities, a keen understanding—a shared sympathy—passed between them. "I'm sorry. You were there, weren't you? When the boy died?"

For a split second, the intensity in those midnight-colored eyes wavered. "That bastard can't go back out on the streets."

"Then let's hope he underestimates me as much as you have tonight."

"Audrey, I… Hell. I shouldn't have opened my mouth." With a deep sigh, those broad shoulders lifted and relaxed a fraction. "You can hang here in the shadows for a minute to get it together, but then I really need you back out by the street."

Was that an apology? Or just a resignation to duty? Either way, after the charged intimacy of their argument, his unexpected capitulation surprised her. She found something calming about his breathing, slowing and evening out along with hers, something soothing in the way he altered his protective stance to stand between her and the world beyond this shadowy hedgerow. She touched the soft blue cotton to her eyes one more time. Even though it was just a bandanna, the old-fashioned gesture charmed her. "I didn't think men carried handkerchiefs anymore."

His soft chuckle warmed her. "You don't know my grandmother. There are rules to follow with the Taylors. Family dinner every Sunday. Men carry handkerchiefs in their pockets."

"Your grandmother tells a tough guy like you what to do?"

He winked, and Audrey felt like smiling, too. "She's my best girl. I do what she asks."

A check of his watch and Audrey suspected the minute to compose herself was up. She held out the bandanna. "Well then, thank her, too."

He wrapped his hand around it and her fingers, holding on longer than necessary to give her a sympathetic squeeze. She was startled by the heat emanating from his skin, even through the protective leather glove he wore. "Keep it. And you get Smith."

Audrey nodded, making a promise.

His grip suddenly tightened and he whirled around, pulling her behind him. A split second later, a camera flashed.

Alex Taylor was already on guard before her own defenses locked into place. "What the hell?"

Another light flashed. He took a menacing step forward.

An older, heavyset man slipped to the side, trying to make eye contact with her. "Miss Kline, could we get a statement?"

Alex shifted his shoulder between her and the reporter, giving Audrey nothing but the large white SWAT letters on the back of his vest to look at. "Get back to the sidewalk, behind the yellow tape."

"Do you think this is the work of the Rich Girl Killer, Miss Kline?"

"The what?"

"I heard her throat was crushed like the other one."

"Oh, my God." The white letters blurred in front of her.

Alex Taylor was moving forward. "I said, back to the street."

She heard another reporter shouting from farther away. "It's Audrey Kline. Over here. Miss Kline, you fit the killer's victimology. Are you worried for your own safety?"

The whirs and clicks of flashing cameras crawled over her skin like an assault of mechanical spiders.

"This is a restricted area. If you don't leave, I'll have you arrested."

"Are you friends with Miss Kline, officer? Why were you holding hands? Is she in danger?"

"I said—"

"I'll handle this." Audrey blinked her vision clear. It was up to her and no one else to pull it together. She touched Alex's arm as she moved beside him, and gave him a squeeze of silent apology for getting dragged into her society-page world. His tricep was as hard and sinewed as his forearm, his skin as warm and reassuring as the grip of his hand had been. But it was time for her to be strong now. "I'll handle this," she repeated, pulling away.

His questioning gaze met hers over the jut of his shoulder. "You don't have to talk to them."

"Who knows what they'll say if I don't?" She stood in front of him, grateful for the wall of heat at her back as the vultures circled around them. "Officer Taylor is securing the scene of a crime. Please respect his orders and move back to the street so that KCPD can do their job and find Gretchen Cosgrove's killer."

"Do you think this death is related to Valeska

Gallagher's unsolved murder? You knew both victims."

"No comment."

"Can you comment on the Demetrius Smith trial?" the heavyset reporter asked.

"Not tonight."

"Are you and—Officer Taylor, is it?—an item?"

That was the news they wanted to report? "One of my best friends was murdered tonight. My love life is not up for discussion."

Audrey startled at the broad hand at the small of her back and the hushed voice against her ear. "Don't let 'em rile you up, Red." And then Alex was reaching around her, moving the reporters back. "Miss Kline has no further comment at this—"

"What are you doing way over here?" The small crowd parted as Harper Pierce nudged his way to the front. Without so much as a nod of acknowledgment to her or Alex, he pulled her hand through the crook of his elbow. "I leave you alone for a few minutes and you get lost."

"Harper." Even in that teasing tone, it felt like a reprimand, as if she was a child.

"Take the help when you can get it," he whispered. He patted his hand over hers, pinning her fingers to his arm so that she couldn't pull away without making a scene and really giving the press something to talk about. "I need you. Gretch's parents want to know if you'd read a statement to the press for them."

"I appreciate the rescue, but I don't think I'm the best person for that right now." But Harper wasn't slowing down. He wasn't taking no for an answer. Maybe he just needed a friend at his side right now. Audrey set aside her own discomfort and summoned compassion. "Of course. Any way I can help."

Although he didn't seem to have the will to smile either, Harper paused with her to allow a picture of the two of them together before escorting her out to the sidewalk. Then his hand was blocking the next camera and they were striding on.

The number of people in the crowd was still growing, and Audrey couldn't help but glance at the technician by the news van, the parking attendant who was retrieving a car for one of the guests, the man in his bathrobe, pajamas and a pair of galoshes on the opposite sidewalk looking on. Alex Taylor said the police suspected that Gretchen's killer was here somewhere, watching the chaotic results of his gruesome handiwork. Had she just brushed past a killer? Been photographed by him? Looked him in the eye? Was it that man? That one there?

Audrey's gaze swept past two young black men, barely out of their teens, if that, lounging against a car at the fringe of the crowd. The shorter one, wearing a white ball cap twisted sideways on his head, leaned over to whisper something to the tall one in a black hoodie. The tall one laughed and looked right at her.

At her.

And then they both raised two fingers and pointed them at her, flicking their thumbs as if they were firing a gun.

"Oh, my God," Audrey gasped. She quickly turned away, missing a step and stumbling into Harper's side.

"Are you all right?" he asked, pausing a moment to help her regain her balance.

What was that about? Did they have something to do with Gretchen's murder? Did those boys know her? Or were they just taking delight in compounding the misery of an easy target?

"I'm fine," she lied, knowing her focus should be on Gretchen and Harper and whatever the Cosgroves needed from her tonight. "I'll be fine."

She looked over her shoulder to see Officer

Taylor herding the reporters who'd found them back to the restricted area. He was watching the two young men who'd mimicked a shooting, too, and was already weaving through the crowd toward them. He looked up from whatever message he was relaying into the radio on his shoulder. She caught one last glimpse of those dark, watchful eyes focused on her before the crowd shifted and he was blocked from view.

Suddenly, she felt oddly alone, even attached to Harper's side in the midst of the crowd. The enormity of potential suspects—of one man, or maybe two—knowing, gloating, getting off on this chaos, closed in on her, constricting her breathing, making her skin crawl. She felt like a specimen under a microscope, completely at the mercy of unknown eyes.

Without really considering the significance of her actions, Audrey shoved the bandanna she still carried into her jeans. She kept her fingers in her pocket, clinging to the one true piece of comfort she'd had since hearing of Gretchen's murder.

Chapter Three

One Month Later

The strains of chamber music muted as Audrey closed the kitchen door behind her. The din of eager, friendly voices from all the polite conversations she'd endured tonight still seemed to echo in her ears, leaving her nearly deaf in the empty room as she breathed a sigh of relief. "That's what I needed."

After allowing herself a moment to savor the quiet, she kicked off her strappy Gucci heels and curled her aching toes against the cool tile, wishing she could shed the fitted gown with the stays that poked into her ribs, as well. But since hostess nudity wasn't the kind of buzz she wanted to generate with this holiday fundraising event, she settled for padding across the kitchen and opening the fridge in search of some caffeine. "Great." She scoped the shelves up and down. "Just great."

Not one diet cola to be found. Coffee? She closed the refrigerator and turned to the empty coffeemaker on the counter.

Out of luck. The only caffeine in the house was on the serving tables the caterers had set up, and she wasn't going back to the party any sooner than she had to. The whole point of sneaking off to the kitchen was to find ten minutes of silence where she could nurse her headache and maybe think a bit more about how she wanted to open her statement to the jury when Demetrius Smith's trial started in the morning.

She already had her arguments lined up. Her evidence was all in order, the witness list approved. Her boss, District Attorney Dwight Powers, had signed off on her strategy for putting away the reputed gang leader. Smith claimed he'd been an innocent bystander as the ten-year-old boy had been shot and killed in his backyard, thinking he could plead out to lesser charges. But Audrey intended to nail him to the wall for a list of crimes ranging from drug-dealing and witness intimidation to Calvin Chambers's murder.

As it did every time she read or thought about the ten-year-old's death, Audrey's memories went back to the night of Gretchen's murder—to the much more personal understanding she now had about violence and innocent lives so cruelly and callously taken. Inevitably, her thoughts of that night ended up at a shadowed hedgerow, where a dark-eyed, opinionated, compassionate cop had given her a few moments of respite from her grief.

You get Smith.

Alex Taylor had angered her, touched her heart, held her hand and handed down an edict.

Right. No pressure.

Apparently, the support of KCPD, as well as career success and personal independence, hinged on winning this trial.

No pressure whatsoever.

No wonder her head ached.

It was Audrey's first big case as a prosecutor. Her chance to prove she was smart enough, gutsy enough and tough enough to win a case without the backing of her father's firm. Rupert Kline expected her to fail and was waiting to pick up the pieces with a hug and a told-you-so. He expected her to come to her senses and accept the lucrative partnership he'd offered in his firm. All his money and influence hadn't been able to save her mother from the cancer that had ravaged her body and ultimately silenced her beautiful spirit. So, by damn, he wasn't going to let anything happen to his little girl.

Even if all that love was smothering her.

So in the kindest, most reassuring way she knew how, Audrey was fighting to be her own woman, to create her own success story—to build her own life that included her father, but wasn't dominated by him. Her mind was more focused, her goals clearer now, than they'd ever been. She didn't need Daddy's money to get the job done. She didn't need his name to give her clout.

She didn't need lectures from some doubting Thomas of a cop, either. She could do this.

She had to do this.

Beyond getting a ruthless criminal off the streets, she needed to succeed in order to prove that, at twenty-seven, with a degree from Smith and a juris doctor from the University of Missouri, she was no longer Daddy's little girl. She was more than the pretty princess in the gilded Kline cage.

So why had she agreed to help her father host this fundraiser for a scholarship to honor Gretchen's memory on the night before the trial began?

Proof that she was her own woman, indeed.

Audrey pulled out a glass and filled it with water from the tap, hating that vulnerable place in her heart. "Why can't I say no to you, Daddy?"

Probably because the arts and friendship were worthy causes. Probably because she was as fiercely protective of her father as he was of her. Audrey had moved back home those last few months when her mother had been ill—to take care of Rupert as much as her mother. Despite the tragedy, Audrey had finally understood what it felt like to be needed. Her. Not her family's money, not her father's name. Her parents had needed their daughter to be there, to love them, to be strong when they couldn't be.

Just like he needed her tonight.

But she really should be practicing her opening statement.

Taking a long drink of water, Audrey pulled out a stool from the counter and sat. Using the center island and the two ovens as her imaginary audience, she began. "Your Honor, ladies and gentlemen of the jury, I'm here today to prove that every citizen of Kansas City deserves justice. Every citizen deserves to feel safe, walking his own streets..." She groaned and shook her head. "Too pompous." She tunneled her fingers beneath the tendrils of hair loosely pinned at her nape and massaged the back of her neck. "No child should live in fear of walking home from school... What's this?"

Lowering her glass, Audrey picked up the sealed envelope lying on top of the basket of pledge cards on the counter. Recognizing the neat handwriting on the front, she smiled. "Charlotte."

Feeling as if she'd just gotten a hug, Audrey slit open the flap and pulled out a note card that was as smart and unassuming as the woman who'd sent it. Charlotte Mayweather was another classmate who'd gone to the same private high school she, Gretchen and Harper Pierce had attended. Audrey tried to remember the last time she'd seen Charlotte—certainly not at Gretchen's funeral. And she hadn't been included on the guest list tonight because Audrey had known she wouldn't be able to come.

Still, as Audrey read the note, she wasn't surprised to see that Charlotte had enclosed a check for the scholarship fund. Somehow, Charlotte had known that they were honoring an old friend tonight. Although she'd never been the social butterfly Gretchen was, Charlotte had always been adamant about supporting the causes—and people—she cared about.

I wish I could be there

the note began.

Like you, Gretchen made a point to come visit me from time to time. She could always make me smile. Here's a token of my affection for her, and how much I miss her. Thanks for doing this for her, Aud.
Good luck with the trial. I'll be following you in the papers.
Charlotte

Good luck? Audrey sighed with a bit of melancholy as she tucked the note and check inside the envelope and dropped it back into the basket. Was there anyone in Kansas City who wasn't watching how she handled the Smith case?

And how many of them expected her to fail?

The swish of the kitchen door sweeping across

the threshold gave her a split-second notice to paste a smile on her face before company joined her. "There you are."

Audrey turned to the distinguished man with the silvering, receding auburn hair and smiled. "Daddy."

"I wondered where you'd gotten off to." He picked up her sandals and carried them over to the counter where she sat. He pressed a kiss to her temple and dropped the shoes into her lap. "No fair skipping out if I can't. Our guests are starting to leave. Will you see them off at the door while I chat up another ten grand from the Bishops?"

"Of course." Pulling up the skirt of her gown, she pinched her feet back into the high heels. She inclined her head toward the basket on the counter. "We received a card with a check from Charlotte Mayweather, too."

"Charlotte? Now there's a name I haven't

heard for a while." He pulled the card from the basket. "How is she doing?"

"I'm not sure," Audrey answered, fastening the delicate buckle at her ankle. "I haven't been to see her lately. But I know she misses Gretchen as much as I do."

"You had a wonderful idea with this scholarship. Gretchen was such a patroness of the arts, it's fitting that she be remembered this way." Audrey knew by his frown that he'd reached the end of Charlotte's note. "Even she knows about this unpleasantness with the Smith trial."

Audrey plucked the card from his hands and returned it to the basket. "That *unpleasantness* is my job. If I win, I'll have the track record to be able to run for district attorney myself one day."

"And if you lose, you'll be vilified by the press. Why don't you come back to Kline, Galloway & Tucker?" *Where I can protect you.*

Where she'd never be anything more than

Rupert Kline's daughter. Or wife to one of his partners, if he had his way. The unspoken arguments were clear and familiar.

But she needed to make her own decisions— captain her own victories and suffer her own mistakes without her father's money or influence to either make them happen or go away. Audrey needed him to know that she was smart enough, capable enough—that *she* was the necessary element to build her own career and find her own happiness, instead of accepting that her life was the result of whatever her father's doting yet misguided love for his only daughter allowed it to be.

Not wanting to tax what energy either of them had left tonight, Audrey wisely changed the subject. "So, are we a rousing success?"

Rupert pulled back the front of his tux and stuffed his hands into the pockets of his tailored wool trousers. "Everyone is interested in giving this time of year. I think Clarice earned her money with this event—pulling it together so quickly and bringing in a lot of donations. She knows how to throw a party."

Did she detect a hint of admiration when her father mentioned the event planner's name? Audrey felt a smile curve her own lips. Her father had been widowed for nearly three years now. If the right woman turned his eye, she wasn't against him seeing where things might lead. A new girlfriend might even distract him from his fixation on her. "Are you and Clarice planning on staying up late tonight to, um, go over some numbers after our guests leave?"

"I may have invited her to stay for a brandy to congratulate her." Rupert took her elbow and helped Audrey to her feet once she was cinched in and ready to report for duty again. He tapped the tip of her nose with his finger and smiled. "But you just put those matchmaking thoughts away, missy. We're only discussing business."

"Does Clarice know that?" As much as she

hated the nickname he'd given her as a toddler, she loved her father even more, and let that argument slide, as well. She laid her palm over his heart, brushing over the bulge of his pacemaker to feel the strong beat of it beneath her hand. "I just want you to know, that if business turns to pleasure, I'll be locked up in my office upstairs, and I won't hear a thing that might go on in your study—or anywhere else on the first floor."

"You're wicked, missy." He scooted her out of the kitchen and Audrey was instantly assaulted by the noise and colors and pressure to be the perfect hostess again. As one of the tallest men in the room, it was easy to spot Harper Pierce when he excused himself from a conversation and headed into the foyer. Harper strode toward them, and Rupert whispered against her ear. "Speaking of matchmaking, I noticed Harper has been sticking close to your side all evening. He knows the board is considering him for a partnership at the firm. Do I give him credit for wanting to date you, or hold it against him?"

"Daddy!" Audrey swatted his arm for teasing her. "Harper was engaged to Gretchen. Don't start throwing him at me before he's done mourning her loss."

He arched one of his silvery-red brows in a paternal warning. "Harper's an ambitious man. I don't know that he'd let grief stand in the way of getting what he wants."

"I don't care for him in that way anymore. He's just a friend—one who's co-hosting this evening's fundraiser with me. That's why he's been so attentive."

"Uh-huh."

"Seriously." Audrey reached up to straighten her father's bow tie. "I'm looking for a man who's a little more into me than he is my daddy's law firm or bank account."

He caught her hands in his and pressed a kiss to her fingers. "I want that for you, too."

Audrey grinned. "And he has to have a personality, support my career, be a good kisser and treat me like a princess."

Rupert laughed. "You don't ask for much, do you? Just promise me you won't be so hard on the boys and focused on success that you wind up all alone."

"That formula worked for you, didn't it?"

"Yes, I found success. But I also found someone to love. I married your mother and had a family."

"I will, too, Daddy." Audrey stretched up on tiptoe to kiss his cheek. "I promise."

As he excused himself to speak with the Bishops, Audrey turned and fixed a smile on her face for Harper's benefit.

"Were you and Rupert talking about me?" Harper asked, his lawyer's voice smooth and concise. Audrey hoped he couldn't feel the flinch that came with automatically steeling herself against the possessive touch around her waist. "I thought I heard something about marriage?"

"Don't flatter yourself, Romeo." Maybe her father was right. Was Harper rebounding from his relationship with Gretchen and setting his sights on becoming more than friends again? Their dates in high school seemed like a lifetime ago and, as far as Audrey was concerned, that was where any romance with him should stay—in the past. Subtly twisting to move his hand to a less intimate position, she pointed to the front door at the far end of the foyer. "I see the Hunts are leaving. I'd better go thank them and say good-night."

"I'll come with you."

Audrey endured a half hour of kisses and handshakes before the ache from her constant smile got a welcome relief from Jeffrey Beecher, the assistant who worked for tonight's event planner, Clarice Darnell.

"Audrey?" Pushing his way through the dwindling crowd, he hurried from the back of the house to join her. The earbud he wore, and wire running down the back of his collar, made her assume the interruption was related to the party. "Audrey, do you have a moment?"

"Sure." She worked the muscles on her face, trying to relax them. "Is there a problem?"

"Can't this wait, Beecher? And you're to address her as Miss Kline."

She stiffened at the unwanted and unnecessary defense on her behalf. "Audrey's fine. What is it?"

He reached inside his suit jacket and pulled out an envelope. "This just came for you."

"At this hour?" Audrey frowned and took the letter. "Maybe it's another donation."

"I don't think so," said Jeffrey. Harper *harumphed* at her side while the hired help monopolized her attention. "A courier delivered it to the service entrance—said to bring it to you immediately. I gave him a five-dollar tip."

Jeffrey pushed up his narrow-framed glasses onto the bridge of his nose and cleared his throat. That was when she realized he was waiting to be reimbursed.

Normally, Audrey would have given him the money herself, but with nothing on but gray silk and lace, and no cleavage to speak of, she had no purse or pockets or hiding place to stash any cash. She turned and rested her hand on Harper's sleeve, dredging up one more smile. "Do you mind?"

"Not for you." Although Harper's enthusiasm faded as soon as he turned his attention away from her, he pulled out his wallet and took Jeffrey aside.

For a delivery that sounded so urgent, the envelope was curiously devoid of red flags or clues as to what the contents might be. A glance through the guests gathering in the foyer indicated an easy exit to the kitchen was out of the question. Staying here meant she'd have Harper looking over her shoulder. Audrey opted for the quickest route to uninterrupted quiet by following the next couple to depart out the front door.

The night air instantly whipped through her hair, giving her senses a reviving shock and raising goose bumps along her arms. There was a dampness to the December breeze, hinting that they'd have a dusting of snow by morning. Perhaps taking a moment to find a wrap for her bare shoulders would have been a smarter move. But she was out here now, the porch was deserted, and the only sounds of company came from the music inside and the crunch of tires over bricks as the valet staff drove up with cars for guests waiting in the driveway below. Hunching her shoulders and shivering against the cold, Audrey moved beneath one of the brass lamps framing the entryway to study the envelope.

Jeffrey was right. It didn't look like any pledge card or personal note regarding tonight's scholarship benefit. There was just her name, typed and neatly centered, along with the address and the courier service logo. No return address, but that was probably included inside. Perhaps it was something from the defense attorney pertaining to Demetrius Smith's case, or a proof of some reporter's column about the pretrial buzz for the newspaper. Trading her society hat for her attorney persona, she opened the envelope and pulled out the enclosed letter to read it.

Her blood chilled.

Oh. My. God.

"You'll catch your death out here, ma'am."

Audrey jumped a mile inside her skin at the voice in the shadows. As the letter floated to the ground, she spun around to locate the balding man in a dark utility uniform climbing the steps onto the porch. Instinctively, she backed against the house at his approach. He was between her and the door now, and he just kept coming.

Her pulse thundered in her ears as she put up her hand. "Stop right there. Please."

That he did what she commanded surprised her even further. With an apologetic nod, he stopped and retreated a step, giving her a chance to calm her nerves and focus in on the name badge pinned to his dark gray parking valet's jacket.

"Bud." She called him by name, recognizing him now as another employee of Clarice Darnell's event staff. "You startled me."

"Sorry about that, ma'am." Fear had given the dampness of the night a chance to sink beneath her skin and she was truly shivering now. "I just wondered if you'd forgotten your coat. I'd be happy to get it for you."

"I'm fine." Audrey rubbed her hands up and down her arms, completely aware that her words belied her actions. He could think her spoiled, an idiot or a liar—she didn't care. She just wanted him to leave. "I got overheated inside.

The fresh air feels good." She pulled away from the chilled moisture of the limestone facade, standing straight and tilting her chin, determined to take control of her emotions. "That'll be all."

Bud, of the thinning brown hair and toothpick he rolled from side to side between his lips, stood beside the porch railing, staring—no, leisurely running his gaze from the goose bumps on her arms along her body right down to her polished toenails. Just when she thought the curious creep might never blink, he bent down and picked up the envelope and letter that had landed between them. "You dropped these."

Audrey snatched the papers from his fingers and tucked them against her stomach. "Thank you."

The tense seconds had stretched beyond uncomfortable when the front door opened beside her. Audrey nodded to the gray-haired couple who stepped outside before catching the door and giving Bud a succinct dismissal. "The Bishops will be needing their car."

"Yes, ma'am. You be careful now. And stay warm." After pushing the knot of his tie up to his collar, Bud took the ticket stub from Dr. Bishop and jogged down the steps onto the circular drive to retrieve their car.

Audrey's "Good night" was for anyone within listening range as she went inside and pushed the door shut behind her.

"Audrey?"

"Not now, Harper." She shrugged off the hand on her arm and marched straight up the carpeted grand staircase. At the top she turned and hurried all the way down the hallway to the circular tower where her bedroom suite and its adjoining office were located.

Even after pulling her dressing gown over her shoulders, she had a hard time feeling any warmer than she had outside. But this wasn't the time to worry about wintry temps or strange men who materialized from the shadows. She locked the bedroom door behind her, grabbed the tweezers from her manicure set to pick up the letter and envelope and went into her office.

Moving her purse from the office chair, Audrey sat and reached for the phone. She needed to call her boss, Dwight Powers, and tell him there'd been a new development in the Smith case. And then she needed to call KCPD.

But she was quickly on her feet again, pacing behind her desk while she punched in the numbers. When the D.A.'s home phone rang, she stopped and took a deep, calming breath. She'd better have her facts straight before she said anything.

Tucking the cordless phone between her shoulder and ear, Audrey flattened the letter on her cherry wood desk and read it again.

She hadn't been mistaken.

No law firm or newspaper logo.

No personal stationery stamp.

No return address.

No name.

Just a threat—as clear as it was anonymous.

It's your turn, Audrey. The others didn't listen to me, but you're a smart girl. Walk away from this trial and go back to your tea parties.

Do the right thing.

Or you'll die doing the wrong one.

"Come on, Dwight. Answer." Her boss had become a family man with his marriage to his second wife and the children that came with that union. Either they'd gone to bed early or they were all out together for a family night. But with each ring of the telephone, the tension inside her wound tighter and tighter.

Who had sent that threat? Although it couldn't have come from Demetrius Smith himself, even kept in isolation from other prisoners, it wouldn't be impossible for a gang leader to get a message out to one of his lieutenants or followers on the outside.

Ring.

Had it truly been a courier delivery? Or had one of Smith's men disguised himself and come to her house? Gotten past security? Been that close to her staff and guests and father?

That close to her?

Was he watching her even now? Learning which bedroom was hers? Enjoying her shell-shocked reaction?

Ring. Ring.

Dwight Powers's voice mail clicked on and Audrey suddenly felt disconnected. Isolated. Alone.

"Suck it up, woman," Audrey chided. She could not—would not—leave a panicked, unprofessional message on her boss's phone.

And then she spotted the blue bandanna— washed and pressed and peeking out of her purse—waiting for a free moment for her to return it with a proper thank-you to its owner, Alex Taylor. She snatched it out of her bag and wrinkled it in her fist, hugging the soft swatch of cotton to her chest.

Alex Taylor's handkerchief had been a gift on one of the saddest nights of her life. His caring gesture—whether motivated by his personal stake in the Smith trial or something chivalrous his grandmother had taught him—had provided an unexpected anchor when she'd been buffeted by a storm of unwanted emotions.

Now she was holding on to it again, clinging to the strength and security it represented.

She wouldn't be scared off this case.

But she was scared.

So, ARROGANT, TOUGH-TALKING Audrey Kline— with all her preaching about being her own woman and setting the world on fire—ran for cover, just like the others.

She could be spooked.

He smiled as he stood in the darkness near the Kline's front gate, watching the imposing rock mansion with its historic architecture and air of refined taste and wealth. He enjoyed being a part of that world. But it was the fear he'd sensed when she'd run into the house that gave him real pleasure tonight.

He exhaled the smoke from his lungs with a deep, satisfied sigh as the lights filtering from her upstairs windows drew his attention. For a moment, he saw her slight figure silhouetted against the interior lights before she quickly moved away from the blinds—as if she knew he was out here—watching, wanting, relishing her distress.

He'd been right about her Achilles' heel. For one woman it had been about protecting her child. For the last one, he'd found it far too easy to prey upon her looks and her fear that once her beauty was gone, she'd have nothing but her money to offer to anyone who might care.

So he'd taken her beauty. He'd struck right at the heart of what terrified her most.

Now, he was free to toy with Audrey Kline. He knew what she wanted—independence, respect, professional success—and he knew how to take it from her.

He'd give her a chance to make things right. Perhaps the smile she'd given him tonight would prove more sincere than the others had been. Everyone deserved a chance.

But if she was playing him…

"I'm still here." He dropped his cigarette and ground it out in the leaves beneath his shoe, turning his attention to the impatient summons on his cell phone. "Yes, I've made all the necessary arrangements," he assured the simpleton who was paying to do his bidding. "I'll take care of everything."

"Is it safe?"

How tedious. "Blowing up anything is never completely safe. But if you follow my directions to the letter and you position yourself where I instructed, then you won't be hurt and you'll have the perfect alibi."

Just as he would.

"You're crazy, man. This better work or I'll be coming after you."

Crazy? His hand curled into a fist down at his side. Although it wasn't the first time he'd heard that word, he'd long ago learned to let the offensive misconception slide off his back. The man on the phone was the real fool if he thought insults or threats could hurt him.

The telltale buzzer of the Klines' security system warned him that the front gate was sliding open and one of the guest's cars was approaching. Forcing his fingers to relax, he backed into the shadows of the ancient oaks that lined the circular drive and blocked him from view of the estate's security cameras.

An unexpected snap froze him into place. It took a therapeutic mantra through his clenched jaw for him to ignore the twig jabbing at his shoulder and retreat another step.

The smooth hum of a finely tuned engine—a Bentley, by the sound of it—passed by before he responded to the nagging insistence of his caller.

"Will it work? Will this freaking plan of yours work?"

He ran his fingers along the broken twig, counting the dry brown leaves that had withered with the change of seasons. "You handle my problem, and I'll take care of yours."

He flipped the phone shut and slipped it into his slacks, pausing a moment before pulling out his pocketknife.

In three strokes, he sawed away the fragmented wood and dropped it to the ground. With one more cut, he sliced off a leaf, leaving two on either side of the branch.

Something eased inside his brain at the symmetry of his handiwork, and he folded the knife and put it away.

Then he plucked his cigarette butt from the ground and stuffed it into his pocket. He straightened his jacket and tie and stepped onto the curving brick driveway, lengthening his stride as he headed to the house. The evening was winding down. It was time for him to get back to his duties before he was missed.

Chapter Four

Winter was in the air. So was something Alex couldn't quite put his finger on.

The powdering of snow that had fallen through the night was still clinging to the grass in the park across the street. Christmas was only three weeks away, but with all the freaks and crazies lined up outside the courthouse that morning, it felt more like Halloween.

Alex handed his gun over to the security guards just inside the lobby of the steel, glass and granite building. He wasn't surprised to see the reporters with their camera crews here to cover the opening day of Demetrius Smith's trial. A car with four of what he guessed were Broadway Bad Boys like Smith was parked beyond the blocked-off street in front of the courthouse. The uniformed officers pulling up in a black-and-white just behind them would check out their IDs and tell the teens and young twenty-somethings to move on.

What Alex didn't expect to see were all the motherly types, religious groups and activists in the park across from the courthouse, with signs of both support and damnation for the proceedings going on inside the building. Some wore colorful coats and banners draped across their chests to draw attention to their cause, he supposed. A few wore stocking masks to remain anonymous. The ghoul dressed up like the Grim Reaper was a little over-the-top, but the message was clear—an innocent child had fallen prey to gang violence, and the moms and grandmas and preachers and papas of Kansas City weren't going to stand for a scumbag like Demetrius Smith roaming their streets and terrorizing their families any longer.

The scar on his back where his Westside Warrior tat had once marked him burned with a mixture of suspicion and guilt. In his early teens, he'd been one of the thugs these people feared. He'd jacked a car once, had done his fair share of vandalism and had proved himself better than a kid should be in a fight. But with his birth mother providing a stellar example of drug abuse, he'd never used or sold the crap and he damn straight had never killed anyone—rival or innocent.

"Sixth floor," the guard instructed, returning Alex's badge.

"Thanks." Tucking the badge into the pocket of his jeans, Alex headed for the elevator. Those same street smarts that had kept him alive when he'd had no one at home to care about his next meal, much less his safety, hummed with an awareness of his surroundings. Something had him on edge. Something he'd seen walking in wasn't right.

Maybe it was just the beefed-up security around the building that made him hypersensitive to his surroundings. The guards monitoring the entrances and exits were routine. But when Alex got off the elevator, the extra uniforms positioned in the hallway and at the courtroom doors reinforced the sense that trouble was hiding someplace close by.

Had there been a threat? Usually, his team was put on notice, whether they were on the clock or not, if any warnings had been called in against the courthouse and its personnel, or if Homeland Security elevated its alert level. Since he was free to come watch the proceedings this afternoon, Alex had to assume that the extra security was simply a precaution with the highly publicized trial—a preemptive warning to dissuade any of those crazies or gangbangers from making a threat in the first place.

But that didn't keep him from wishing he still had his Glock on his belt as he shrugged out of his black leather jacket and showed his ID to the guard who let him in the courtroom's thick mahogany doors.

Once inside, Alex easily spotted Trip's wide shoulders and slipped into the aisle seat beside him.

"You're late, shrimp," the big man whispered.

"Told you I was moving some furniture out of storage for my grandparents this morning. I offered to let you help."

Trip grinned. "No, thanks. I thought somebody better keep an eye on Sarge today."

"I can hear you talking." Although Sergeant Delgado seemed to have taken Calvin Chambers's death especially hard, he wasn't above joining the sotto voce fray and putting his men in their places. "Shh."

Obeying the command, Alex took a minute to identify all the players in the room. Judge Grover Shanks was an imposing figure at the bench. Audrey Kline—pure class in her navy-blue suit, with her auburn hair pinned at her nape—stood at the table several rows in front of Alex. She was in a heated debate with Cade Shipley, a defense attorney he recognized as much from his press coverage as from Alex's few appearances in the courtroom. Shipley stood beside a seated black man wearing a charcoal pinstripe suit. Even from the back, there was no mistaking Demetrius Smith's shaved head, gold earring and bored slouch.

Alex's skin tingled with awareness. Smith looked more like a rap star at an awards show than the bleeding bastard they'd hauled out of his drug house in a black, skintight hoodie and handcuffs. Just one more thing that wasn't as it should be today.

Alex turned to Trip. "What's with all the uniforms in the building?"

"I'm not sure. Something's hinky, but I haven't heard anything official or seen anything out of place."

Good. So he wasn't the only one bothered by that intangible air of lurking danger. "How's it going?"

Sergeant Delgado offered a surly whisper. "The D.A.'s office is gettin' their butt kicked. Kline made a great opening statement, but it's been downhill ever since."

Alex leaned against the arm of his seat, giving himself a clear line of sight straight down the center aisle. The mention of butt kicking drew his focus to Audrey's sweet, round bottom.

Sucker. Why couldn't his unguarded thoughts this past month be filled with a woman who wasn't quite so far out of his league?

But no, he had to notice. As icily untouchable as the rest of her might be, there was an earthy sway about that backside that was as distracting in sedate navy-blue wool today as it had been in hip-hugging jeans that night at the Cosgrove estate.

More than once, he'd wondered how she'd dealt with the intrusion of all those reporters that night. How was she coping with her grief? Burying it the way he'd seen her lock down control over her fears and vulnerability when the cameras had started flashing? Had the tall blond suit who'd claimed ownership over her given her a shoulder to cry on? Steered her away from the two thugs who'd pretended to shoot her? Alex ignored the little twinges of jealousy and contempt, and smiled inside. Did she ever find a powder puff to help her mask her pink-tipped nose and the all-too-human evidence of emotion that had reddened her eyes and splotched her cheeks? She'd been so self-conscious about him seeing her like that. Okay, so he'd gone looking for the trespasser he'd heard and found a frightened, upset woman instead. She'd argued with him and he'd pressured her about this trial. Still, remembering her with her guard completely stripped away like that—clinging to his hand, holding on to him—felt...intimate.

Dutifully ignoring the appreciative heat licking through his veins, Alex lifted his gaze to the defiant tilt of her head and tuned in to a voice that was much sharper than the raw huskiness he remembered. "Your Honor, my esteemed colleague, Mr. Shipley, seems to think he has an open-and-shut case."

"The burden of proof is on you, Miss Kline." Shipley's voice was nothing short of patronizing as he turned his dark eyes on Audrey. "While my client admits to being on the scene of the standoff with KCPD's SWAT team and drug task force, he, in fact, was an innocent bystander who was also injured."

Tanya Chambers's gasp echoed through the courtroom, drawing Alex's attention to the second row where she sat weeping, squeezing the arm of the older woman beside her. That took a lot of gall to compare Smith's flesh wound to the bullets that had killed a ten-year-old boy. A buzz of commentary instantly erupted among the crowd. Alex heard everything from words of sympathy for the boy's mother to accusations of, "Innocent, my ass" and a "Shut it" that identified where two young men from Demetrius's Broadway Bad Boy posse were sitting.

"Quiet!" Judge Shanks rapped his gavel on his bench. "This courtroom will be silent or it'll be empty. Do I make myself clear?"

As the comments quickly quieted, Audrey turned to give Tanya Chambers an apologetic smile. Whatever she was about to say died on her lips when those bright green eyes locked on Alex. Her pale cheeks flushed with color as he held her gaze. But before he could even offer a thumbs-up, she turned to face the judge again, quickly reaching into the briefcase on her chair and shoving something down inside.

That woman was a puzzle. Icy cool and smokin' hot. She wore her emotions on her skin yet denied feeling them with every tightly articulated word. "All I'm asking for is a short continuance to reinterview—"

"If Miss Kline's star witness is unable to testify—"

"The witness Mr. Shipley is referring to was found shot to death in his home this weekend, Your Honor." Alex could imagine the accusatory glare she turned on Cade Shipley and the defendant at his table. "If your client knows anything about Trace Vaughn's murder—"

"Objection." Demetrius shook his head while his lawyer defended the insinuation. "The prosecution is making a prejudicial statement about my client. Mr. Vaughn was a known gang member. His unfortunate death is under investigation by KCPD, and no arrests have been made as of yet. Mr. Smith has been in a jail cell since his arrest, so he has an airtight alibi. He is not involved in that crime."

The ribbing chatter from the two thugs in attendance was quickly silenced with a look from the judge and the approach of one of the uniformed guards. Well, son of a gun. Did those two boys look familiar?

Audrey continued to argue her point. "Demetrius Smith also has an affiliation with the Broadway Bad Boys—"

"If that were the case, he'd hardly promote the shooting of one of his own people."

"He could order—"

Judge Shanks pounded his gavel. "The objection is sustained. Jurors will disregard any mention of the defendant's alleged knowledge of Vaughn's murder." He turned from the twelve people in the box at the front of the room to point his gavel at Audrey. "If you can prove a connection between Mr. Vaughn's death and the proceedings at hand, I'll reconsider your motion for a delay, Miss Kline. Until then, do you have enough evidence to proceed with the prosecution?"

Was Smith grinning? Alex sat up straight in his seat. He couldn't read the bastard's expression from this angle, but there was no mistaking that Demetrius was looking straight across the aisle at Audrey, no doubt daring her to make good on her promise to put him away. What the hell? He curled his fingers into his palm, fighting the urge to wipe that smirk off his face. Couldn't the judge see that?

Audrey apparently did. Whatever message had been silently communicated, she shrugged it off, tilted her chin to that arrogant angle and faced the judge. "Yes, Your Honor. The D.A.'s office is ready to continue with its case against Demetrius Smith."

"Very well." The judge tucked his papers into a folder and closed it before striking his gavel one last time. "Court is recessed for this afternoon. We'll reconvene at 9:00 a.m. tomorrow. Bailiff, will you escort the jury out."

"All rise."

Alex stood with everyone else as the judge exited to his chambers and the jurors followed the bailiff through a door at the front of the room. With the sudden buzz of conversations and movement of people filing into the aisle, it was impossible to make out the exact words being exchanged up front. But Demetrius Smith was tall enough that Alex could see his focus on Audrey. And as two guards turned him and took him away, Alex saw the slight nod of his head out into the crowd. His two bros shouted something in return.

His body tensed and ready to spring, Alex stepped into the path of the two young gang-bangers, reading their faces as they approached, trying to figure out what coded communication had just passed between them and Demetrius.

Every gang had their own set of hidden signs, colors, words, symbols that could say anything from "I belong here" to "You're dead." But there were a few messages that remained universal between gangs and generations of gang members—even when they went on to become cops.

Alex widened his stance, breathed in deeply and claimed the path leading to the exit. Both boys were teens, maybe twenty. Both were taller, skinnier, than Alex. And both understood Alex's silent warning.

"What?" the first one said, stopping in his tracks, giving Alex his space. "You harassin' us, officer?"

So they did remember him chasing them away from the Gretchen Cosgrove murder scene.

"We ain't done nothin'," the second one said, pulling on a white ball cap before turning it to the side and tipping up the brim. "We's just here for a friend."

"What did Demetrius say to you?"

"Nothin'."

Alex wasn't playing games with these wise guys. "What did you say to him?"

If he stood there long enough, waited long enough, intimidated long enough, one of them would crack. The first one did. "We told D he was gonna get off."

"Any particular reason you'd say that?"

"Cuz there's this guy—"

"Shut up." The second teen took off his hat and whacked his buddy on the shoulder. So Hat Boy was the brains of the duo. He was smart enough to know when to cut and run, at least. "We ain't doin' nothin' wrong bein' here, officer."

"You're the boys I chased off that murder scene in Mission Hills. You wouldn't be stalking Miss Kline, would you? Intimidating the opposing counsel is a crime, you know."

The teen in the white cap put up his hands in mock surrender. "Hey. We's just here to support

D. We ain't said nothin' to your lady friend. Are we free to go?"

With a nod, Alex stepped aside, knowing he wouldn't get anything else out of them now. "Be good," he warned.

Hat Boy slapped his friend in the back of the head, reprimanding him on their way out the door. Alex watched White Hat turn to the right, away from the elevators, as he pulled on his jacket.

He tapped on Trip's arm, interrupting his conversation with Sergeant Delgado. "Don't go anywhere for a while, okay?"

"You onto something, shrimp?"

"I want to check those two out. Sly and Twitch is how they introduced themselves last time. Call it in and see if you can get me their names. Turn on your phone and I'll keep you posted." Then he was weaving through the crowd, hurrying to follow the two members of Demetrius's crew through the closing steel door of the stairwell exit.

Alex caught the door and slipped inside onto the landing. He hugged the painted cinder-block wall, listening to the sounds of footsteps running down the stairs. Those boys would have been patted down for guns or knives before they even got past the front door. But that didn't mean they couldn't have found a way to stash something in the stairwell—not if there was some *guy* with a plan for them to make Smith a free man again. But the rhythm of their steps was even, continuous. They weren't stopping to arm themselves.

Alex took off down the stairs behind them, moving as quickly as he could without making a sound. Sly and Twitch were crossing the lobby when Alex came through the stairwell door behind them. They had no visible weapons, but Sly with the hat was on his cell phone before he even got out the door. They broke into a jog as soon as they were outside, skirting the crowd of reporters waiting on the sidewalk out front. Alex went to the glass and watched them run up to the corner, where a dark red Impala pulled up. The two got in and the car sped away. It was different from the car he'd seen on his way in. That was a lot of Triple Bs out of their neighborhood at one time. Could something be going down if they were all driving away?

He let his gaze slide across the street to the park. Maybe a third of the people there were wearing some sort of low-slung hat or mask—ostensibly to keep out the cold, but conveniently keeping them from being identified, as well. That'd be an easy enough way to gather enough numbers for an attack of some kind. But no, subterfuge wasn't a gang's way. They were about an in-your-face show of strength and violence.

Alex stood at the window a few moments longer, watching, thinking—wishing he could pinpoint exactly what felt out of place here. The protesters clamored behind the line where they were allowed to congregate. Some of them just wanted their moment on TV; others were taking a stand. Mothers armed with placards. Preachers having their say. The Grim Reaper.

Maybe it was just that guy's poor taste in attention-grabbing garb that made Alex think there was more than the usual trial hoopla going on here.

The elevator dinged on the far side of the lobby and when the doors opened, the noise level inside the building doubled. Audrey, wearing a green trench coat and carrying her leather shoulder attaché, stepped out. Her red hair seemed like a beacon that the security guard, Cade Shipley, a group of print reporters and others followed out. While another guard escorted Mrs. Chambers and her friend toward a quieter side exit, Audrey, Shipley and the reporters all filed through the security gate at the front entrance.

The instant the front doors opened, the press contingency outside swarmed upon them. They split into two groups, some following Shipley's tall, dark, smooth-talking sales pitch, while others circled Audrey until she was hidden from view.

Hidden didn't sit well with Alex. So what if she was a striking, recognizable face from the Kansas City society page who could sell papers and give a cogent interview? Their eagerness to get a piece of Audrey's attention felt more like ganging up on her, as if she was trapped, as if they didn't give a damn about the invasion of her personal space or the job she was trying to do.

Even if that job didn't involve winning a case that was of personal importance to his team, every save-the-day instinct that had been drilled into him since the Taylors had adopted him and inspired him to protect and serve in the first place screamed at him to help out the lady. It took just over a minute for him to check out with the guard and collect his gun, and another thirty seconds to clip his badge on his belt and get through the door.

Catching up to Audrey's group was easy. Spotting her in the middle proved a little more difficult. What he wouldn't give for the eight inches Trip had on him in height right about now.

But what he couldn't see, he listened for. He tuned in to Audrey's voice and politely pushed his way toward the sound. "I got the jury I wanted picked this morning—more women than men. They should be sympathetic to our side of the case."

He almost grinned when he saw her red hair. She talked as if she was holding court, but there was nothing to smile about when he saw her effort to move forward, to get through them with little success. The uniformed officer who'd escorted her out kept the crowd at arm's length, but they weren't letting her pass.

A reporter who identified himself as Steve Lassen, an independent journalist, asked, "Did your office do anything to protect your witness, Trace Vaughn? Lining him up to testify against his former boss got him killed, don't you think?"

That was when Audrey's chin jerked up, a signal Alex was beginning to think meant someone had struck a nerve. "Mr. Vaughn wasn't the prosecution's only witness."

"But the fact you subpoenaed him to testify signed his death warrant, right? Any regrets over the deal you made with him?"

Audrey's steps stuttered to a halt. "I can't comment on an ongoing police investigation."

Alex gave up on being polite and pushed his way through to the center of the mikes and cameras encircling her. With a nod toward the officer beside her, he slipped an arm around her waist. At her startled gasp, he latched on to a handful of her coat and pulled her into the crowd. "Miss Kline has answered all the questions she can for now."

"What are you doing?" She tried to pry his fingers loose.

"Giving you a chance to breathe."

"Miss Kline…" Another round of questions bombarded them, and rethinking her resistance to his rescue, Audrey leaned her shoulder into his chest and hastened her stride to match his. His strong arm and stern look cleared a path for them and he got her through the crowd and onto the street.

"Thank you," she said, pulling away from Alex. She adjusted the strap of her bag on her shoulder, clutching it between them like some kind of shield. "I never used to be claustrophobic, but sometimes, when they're all shoving a camera in my face—"

"Keep moving."

One look at the throng of protesters and well-wishers waiting in the park on the opposite side of the street for their chance to be heard, and Alex claimed her waist again. Snugging her to his side, he angled their path up the hill to the intersection and empty sidewalk there. She fit nicely, just the right height for his five feet ten inches, even in those high heels that tapped across the pavement. But if she'd noticed the way her rounder hips butted against his harder angles, she wasn't savoring the contact the way he was.

Instead, she was fighting him. "I don't appreciate your caveman tactics, Mr. Taylor. Those reporters are just doing their job."

She wanted caveman? Alex stopped in his tracks, his left hand the only thing that kept her from pitching forward. His right hand settled on the opposite side of her waist and he turned her in his arms, letting her read the warning in his eyes. "And they're keeping you from doing yours."

"Yes, I'm very well aware that you and your

friends were there to check up on me—to see if I could do my job or not." Her green eyes sparked and she flattened her palm against his chest, pushing some distance between them. Even through the jacket and knit shirt he wore, the unexpected touch singed his skin. Probably not the reaction she was going for. Not the one he needed to be feeling right now, when he was trying to maintain the upper hand and get her away from the crowd.

"Don't flatter yourself, Red. We weren't spying on you. But two of Smith's thugs were."

"What?"

"I thought so. The two thugs who threatened you at the Cosgrove murder scene?" Easily overpowering both her hand and that tongue, he tucked her back to his side and crested the hill, checking the crossroads in all four directions. The uniforms were keeping the protesters in the park. The lights kept the downtown traffic moving in a normal pattern. He nodded to the surface parking on one corner, and the parking garage on another. "Where's your car?"

"Two blocks down. At the D.A.'s office."

"Are you kidding? You're walking to your office?"

"*We're* walking the two blocks if you don't let me go."

Smart mouth.

"I always walk if the weather's nice. The snow has melted off the sidewalks—the wind isn't bad. The fresh air and exercise clear my head. Are you sure those were the same boys?"

So much for a quick escape, putting his conscience to rest and getting on with the rest of his life.

"Fine. Don't make this easy." He took her hand and veered south along the sidewalk, heading for the yellow limestone high-rise across the street from the far end of the park. She wanted to walk? Then she could hustle up those expensive shoes and keep pace with him before they got cornered by somebody else. "For your information, we were at the courthouse to support Mrs. Chambers and Sergeant Delgado. Her son died in his arms, and he's not dealing with it very well. We're a team—we stick together. We're always there to back up the other. Frankly, you looked like you were fighting that battle all on your own."

Speaking of backup, he owed Trip a call or text message. Alex's instincts had been right about sensing trouble; it just hadn't come from the source he'd expected. But he wasn't about to tell Trip Jones that he was going toe-to-toe with a stubborn woman who was testing his patience. No, sir. An admission like that would only trigger another six months of giving the rookie grief.

"I know what I'm doing, Officer Taylor," Audrey insisted. "I'm not afraid of a fight."

"You prove that to me every time we meet."

She dug in her heels and jerked her hand from his grip. "Officer—"

"It's Alex." He spun around, sparing a glance beyond her shoulder to see a few members of the press sizing up this standoff between the police and the D.A.'s office to see if something newsworthy was about to happen. But it was hard to look away from pink creeping into Audrey's cheeks. "All I'm saying is that maybe you need to fight a little smarter. Maybe a little less guttin' it through on attitude, and using a little more common sense." The blush of temper faded and her gaze dropped to the base of his throat. He'd struck a nerve with that last observation. Hell. That hadn't been his intention. So all that high-and-mighty society arrogance *was* a defense mechanism. "I'm just making a point."

Her gaze shot back to his. "That I lack common sense?"

"That you're not as tough as you try to be." The breeze whipped a tendril of fiery hair across her pale cheek. Alex caught it with his fingertip and brushed it back into place across her cool skin. He tucked the strand behind her ear, entranced by the warmth that colored her cheek beneath his touch. He exhaled a steadying breath, fighting the temptation to press his lips to the same spot to find out how responsively her skin would react.

But a flash of movement caught his eye at the same time she cleared her throat to break the tender mood. The protesters in the park were drifting this way, following Steve Lassen and his camera as the reporter decided there might be a story in trailing Audrey, after all. Although Lassen was twenty yards away and the protesters were following a parallel course through the park's walkways, they were getting entirely too close for Alex's liking.

He grabbed Audrey's hand and pulled her into step beside him. "C'mon."

This time he slowed his pace so it wouldn't look so much like they were running away. Audrey seemed to respond to the concession.

She laced her gloved fingers through his and lengthened her stride to keep up. "Just because you've caught me at a couple of low moments in my life doesn't mean I lack the skills to be a good attorney who can make a difference in this city."

"I'm not knocking your skills, Red." He pulled his phone from his pocket and punched in Trip's number. "I just think you lack a backup plan."

"And you're it?"

He glanced across his shoulder at her sarcasm. "Did you want to be stuck in the middle of all that?"

"All right. Fine. Thank you," she conceded. "But this is a one-time rescue. I'll be better prepared for all this chaos tomorrow. I wasn't expecting this kind of publicity. I'll just transfer everything I've learned about being in the spotlight with my personal life over to my work."

"I'm not talking about losing your temper and having it splashed all over the news, or getting claustrophobic in a crowd—I'm talking about your safety. If something happens to you, this trial gets delayed or dismissed."

"My safety? Did you not see the security at the courthouse?"

"Where is it now?" He swung his arm wide, gesturing to the entourage following them through the park. That Reaper creep with his painted face and hooded robe was moving along with the crowd, as well. That guy had some serious issues. Alex texted a message to Trip and pocketed his phone. "You've got dozens of people following you—"

"In broad daylight." She pointed to the two officers keeping the crowd in their designated area along the park paths. "Surrounded by cops. It's only two blocks from the courthouse to my office. What could anyone do?"

Was she serious? Open ground surrounded by tall buildings or crowded parking lots? Her bright auburn hair was as good as a target out here. And situations were almost impossible to control when there were this many people thrown into the mix. "Those cops are focused on the crowd, not you. Next time, you should arrange to have a car pick you up. And you definitely shouldn't make this walk on your own, not while the trial's going on."

"We're behind you, Audrey!" a voice yelled from the park.

Others joined in. "Keep our children safe!"

"We're counting on you!"

Audrey raised her hand to wave. Alex snatched it back down to her side and her smile for her fans turned into a scowl for him. "See? They know I work for them, not some high-priced law firm like Cade Shipley. They're on my side."

"Is that what this is about? Proving you're a woman of the people?" Alex kept walking. "You're giving the press and everyone in the park who are dying to have their voice heard a

golden opportunity to question or harass you—
or something worse."

"They have a right to be here. They're fright-
ened for their children and their community.
They want me to understand that message.
They're supporting me."

"What if one of them thinks you're not doing
the job the way they want? Or you're not doing
it fast enough to suit them?"

"They're not…"

Alex heard the squeal of tires and instinctively
put his hand on his gun and put himself between
Audrey and the street. "Stay back."

Red car. Speeding toward them. Dark windows except for the one sliding down.

"Alex?" She tugged at his sleeve.

He pulled his weapon, steadied it between
his hands. His finger brushed the trigger, but
he lowered his gun at the last second. The car
slowed as something sailed through the open
window, but no one was shooting.

"You scared yet, bitch?"

Alex spun, reaching for her. But he was a split second too late. "Audrey!"

Something red and juicy struck her jaw and the side of her neck. A tomato.

She was stunned, but not hurt. The mess was dripping under her white collar and onto her coat, and she was pissed. She wiped the biggest glob of mushy pulp from her face and walked over to the trash can at the curb to flick it inside. "Are they kidding me with this?" She pulled a piece of the skin from her lapel. "Who throws tomatoes?"

"Are you hurt?" Alex didn't know whether to touch her or not. He ID'd the make of the car and read a partial plate before the first picture snapped. "You're gonna be front-page news if I don't get you out of here now." *Definitely touch her.* "Audrey?" Pointing his gun down at his side, he reached for her with his left hand. His eyes were scanning, assessing. Car gone, around the corner at the next block and out of sight. Uniforms closing in. Press closing in. Crowd…

"We need to move, Red."

And then he heard the beep from the trash can.

"Get down!"

Alex picked her up around the waist and threw her to the ground across the sidewalk. He dove on top of her, shielding her with his body as the trash can exploded into shards of molten plastic and flying metal and rained down around them.

"Oh, my God. Oh, my God."

It took a few seconds for Alex's stunned hearing to adjust to the sound of Audrey's voice. He felt the throb of pain in his hand and the pinch of her fingers digging into his forearm through his jacket and sweater before he clearly heard the distress in her tone. The quick recovery time for his ears meant the bomb hadn't been that big, or else the concussive blast would have done more damage.

Nothing else on him was hurting beyond some bruised knuckles and a scrape above the band of his watch. He pushed himself up on his elbows, easing the crush of his body over hers. But he wasn't quite ready to free her. "Audrey, are you hurt?"

"Skinned my knee, maybe." She had a nice red welt on her cheek that was starting to ooze blood. But she didn't seem to notice her own injuries. Or care. "Is anyone else hurt?" She pushed at him with her hips, and he let her roll over and sit up while he knelt beside her. Like him, she surveyed the others, hunkered close to the ground—a few with some minor scrapes, one woman was holding her head—nothing that looked like a shrapnel wound, though. Some were in shock. "Is everyone okay?"

One officer was helping a woman to her feet. Another was on his radio. Good. Help was coming. As a police officer, he was supposed to be responsible for all these people, too. But his concern was focused solely on Audrey. Her hair had fallen loose from its pins and he brushed it away from her injured cheek. "Doesn't look like anything serious," he reassured her. "I'm sure backup and ambulances arc already on their way."

She tilted her wide green eyes to his. "Is this my fault?"

"Don't go there." He holstered his gun as he turned to inspect the pattern of debris around what was left of the trash can. The blast area was small and localized, indicating that the goal of the explosion wasn't to do a lot of damage. It was meant to do *specific* damage. To a specific person? Alex looked back to Audrey, hating the suspicion pouring into his veins. "Whoever set that off is the one you should blame."

He heard the click of a camera and whirled around, on his feet, his hands curled into fists. "Get out of here, Lassen."

The heavyset man with a receding hairline

and shrewd eyes shook his head. "Someone tries to kill Rupert Kline's daughter, and you don't think that's front-page news?"

Audrey's fingers pulled at Alex's, opening his fist as she pulled herself up beside him. "How much would it cost to buy that picture back, Mr. Lassen?"

"Are you kidding? This could get me back full-time at the paper, lady. No sale."

She wrapped her arm through Alex's and held on, although he wondered if she was shielding herself or sensing the tension roiling through him and keeping him in check. "You go have a nice career, Mr. Lassen. Just remember…" her tone was in full lawyer mode now "…you're trespassing on a crime scene. If you don't clear out of here right now, I'll have this fine officer arrest you."

Go, Red.

Lassen swore. Then swore again. "You big shots with all your money—you think you own this town. But you don't. I have every right to make my living, and you can't—"

"You really want to threaten her with me standing here, Lassen?" The instant the reporter took half a step forward, Alex planted himself squarely in his path.

"Are you the bodyguard or the boyfriend?" Was that going to be part of his story?

Alex faked a lunge forward. Lassen stumbled backward, cursing cocky cops and daddy's girls and life in general as he turned and stormed up the sidewalk.

Audrey wiped another swath of tomato juice from her neck. "You'd better brace yourself. We are so hitting the rumor mill tomorrow."

"That doesn't bother me." He picked up her attaché bag and handed it to her, steaming at the knowledge that that wasn't only juice trickling over her skin.

Just after the blast, the Reaper had been standing there in the park, watching. Now he was gone. That bothered him even more than the reporters who were finally on the scent of Lassen's story and hurrying along the sidewalk toward them. It bothered him more than the bomb.

"Should we go?" Audrey prompted.

The roar of a heavy-duty truck engine gunning down the hill was the best news Alex had had since leaving the courtroom. Backup had arrived. He hooked his fingers around her arm. "Yeah. Going is good."

Rafe zoomed up to the curb in his black pickup truck. Trip opened the passenger door and jumped out before they came to a complete stop. "We came as soon as we got your text and could get out of the garage. What the hell's going on?"

"Bomb in the trash can. More for effect than to do any real damage. Remote detonation. Could have been the kids in the car, could have been, hell…could have been anybody." Audrey tilted her chin up—way up—and sidled closer to Alex as he pulled her past Trip. "I need her out of here. Now."

Trip swung around at the approaching footsteps of a dozen curious onlookers and eager reporters. "I got this. Meet you back at HQ." He raised his badge in the air, his booming voice taking command of the scene. "KCPD. Stop right where you are. Everybody remain calm and do exactly what I say."

There wasn't a bigger wall between Audrey and potential danger than Trip Jones. But she braced her hand against the door frame and refused to climb in. "Wait a minute. I thought we were walking." They didn't have control of the scene yet and Alex wasn't in the mood to argue. He spanned his hands around her waist and lifted her into the cab, pitching her into the middle of the seat and climbing in behind her. "What are you doing? You're kidnapping me now? Who are you people?"

"SWAT Team One. That was Trip. This is Rafe." Alex pulled the door shut. "Go, Sarge. D.A.'s office. Unless you want to hit the emergency room first?" he asked her.

Audrey shook her head, sinking back into the seat between them as Rafe put the truck into gear and called Dispatch on the radio.

"I was in control of my life half an hour ago. What's happening?" She opened her attaché on her lap and pulled out a blue bandanna.

His blue bandanna.

After all this time she was still carrying that old rag with her?

As she pulled open her coat to clean some tomato drippings from her collar bone, Alex plucked the bandanna from her hand. He heard her soft gasp of breath and watched the self-conscious heat creep along her neck. When his eyes met hers, he tried to communicate that he had no problem with her holding on to his gift from that night of the murder.

Her eyes never left his as he pinched her chin between his thumb and forefinger, and angled her face to dab at her wound. He hoped she could read the same confusion in his eyes. He didn't get this connection between them, either, but it was there. Whether she wanted to argue or let him touch her gently like this, the connection was there.

The reality of knowing she could have been hurt so much worse by that bomb was there, too.

He held up the bandanna and let her see the blood. Her blood.

"I think somebody just made their voice heard."

Chapter Five

"Are you sure you're all right?"

Her blouse was ruined and the strawberry mark scraped across Audrey's cheek throbbed with every anxious beat of her pulse, but she hardly wanted to confess that to her boss. "I'm fine."

Dwight Powers stood behind his walnut desk, buttoning his suit coat and straightening his tie. "I'll take over the case."

That was exactly what she'd been afraid this meeting was about. "No." She shot up out of her chair and mirrored his stance across the desk.

"That's what this person wants—to intimidate me right out of that courtroom." *You scared yet, bitch?* The words had gotten under her skin when she'd been crushed beneath Alex's body and the world had exploded all around them. But she couldn't let them get inside her head. "If I don't finish what I've started here, I'll never have authority over anything in this office again. No one in this city will trust me to protect them."

"An anonymous threat is one thing. Getting close enough to actually hurt you is something different." Dwight trailed a finger across the photo of his second wife and family framed on top of his desk before raising his probing gaze back to her. "I know what it's like to lose people you care about because of this job. No career is worth that."

Audrey fisted her hand on top of the desk. "Demetrius Smith is not going to get to me."

"He got to Trace Vaughn."

"We don't know that."

"Audrey—"

She threw up her hands and spun away, pacing around the guest chairs and collecting her thoughts before returning to the desk. "I realize that's the most likely scenario—the one KCPD is pursuing—that one of his Bad Boys took out Trace. But that has yet to be proved. Think about this logically. Think about Kansas City, not just me."

"I have to think about the people who work for me. You're my responsibility as much as the people we represent."

As tough and overprotective as her boss could be, she knew he could be reasoned with if her arguments were all in place.

With a deep sigh through his barrel chest, he pulled back the front of his suit jacket and propped his hands at his waist. "But I'm listening."

Audrey calmed her breathing, as if she was

making a final summation to a jury. "I know you agreed to give me this assignment because the Kline name carries more legal clout than the other A.D.A.s can bring to the table. You considered the public relations message surrounding this case—city officials and the movers and shakers will see the Kline name and think you're bringing out the big guns to go up against gang violence in K.C."

"You *are* a 'big gun' in my office." Dwight folded his arms across his chest. "But your last name isn't the only reason I gave you this case."

"Exactly." Audrey had given up on her hair staying pinned into place, and had simply combed the waves down around her shoulders. Now she tucked it behind one ear and tilted her head, bringing the mark on her cheek into focus. "You're also counting on that intangible sympathy vote from the jury. If things are close, you're hoping they'll look at little ol' me—too skinny and too pale—standing up against a bully like

Smith and his high-priced lawyer, and they'll vote for the underdog."

"That strategy won't do me any good if my *underdog* gets hurt and can't finish the trial."

"You're going to make my point for me, sir." Time to reel him in. "Any delays or a switch in counsel after today's opening statements makes our office look weak. A shark like Cade Shipley would jump all over that and sway the jury. If we're not ready to prove our case, if a rookie like me can't prove it—"

"You're too sharp to ever think like a rookie. Why do you think I hired you?"

"Thanks. But if you're going to believe in me, *believe* in me. Let me do this." Audrey was beat-up and tired, but she wouldn't reduce herself to begging. Yet she could tell he wasn't quite convinced that she could win—or maybe even survive—this case. "I have a ton of circumstantial evidence to present."

"That will convict him on lesser charges

where he'll pay a fine and walk in a couple of years. I want that murder charge to stick."

"The lab can prove the bullet that killed Calvin Chambers came from the gun registered to Smith."

"Smith claims he couldn't find his gun that day, that it was stolen or one of his boys must have been using it. He had no GPR on him or his clothes. You need a witness to put that gun in his hand."

"Then I'll find one. I convinced Trace to turn on Smith for a reduced sentence. I'll find someone else to do the same."

"You know what you're saying, Audrey? You're talking about going into no-man's-land to meet with gang members on their turf—or sitting down in a room with them one-on-one. You're putting pressure on young thugs who'd rather chew you up and spit you out than cooperate." He swiped his palm across the top of his silver and blond hair and cursed. "And if you're not scared of Demetrius's threats, they will be."

"If this job was easy, I wouldn't have been interested in it." She could hear other attorneys and staff members outside Dwight's door closing down their offices and cubicles for the day. But she wasn't ready to quit on this. "I need to be in that courtroom tomorrow morning, Dwight. Please. Maybe if I show a little courage, I'll inspire a witness to show a little courage and come forth, too."

The D.A. scratched his head, frowned, cursed. But he knew she was right. "All right. You're still on the case."

"Thank you." The urge to run around the desk and hug him sparked through her muscles. But that would negate the image of strength she'd just sold him, so she settled for a grateful smile and headed for the door.

"But…"

Oh, the power of a single word. Relief curdled

into frustration and made her wary. She slowly turned to find out what the catch was. Co-counsel? Direct supervision from the boss himself? "But?"

"I want you to have round-the-clock protection."

"We have a state-of-the-art Gallagher Security system installed at home. And there are guards all over the courthouse and this building."

"I'm talking about a bodyguard. Someone who's with you 24/7. From what I understand, that bomb went off when you were nowhere near a security team." He picked up the phone. "I'm calling KCPD."

A bodyguard? Now she'd really look like the spoiled rich girl who bought her own protection while the rest of the city—like those people in the park this afternoon, or Mrs. Chambers—had to face the dangers of this world on their own. She hurried to the desk and pushed the disconnect button. "The city can't afford that."

"It's not negotiable, Audrey. If Smith and his gang can get to someone from my office, that's the ultimate intimidation. This city will never feel safe again. And I won't stand for them hurting one of my people." He hung up the receiver and snapped his fingers, a man with a purpose striding out his office door. "I've got an idea."

Audrey followed him through the doorway, as curious as she was worried about the next kink someone else was going to throw into her life.

Dwight crossed straight past the empty cubicle stations to her tiny office. A compact, raven-haired man got up from the chair behind her desk and met them at the open door. A badge hung from a steel chain around his neck. The gun at his waist looked as dangerous as the broad stretch of his shoulders.

Oh, no. No, no, no. Audrey hurried to catch up.

Dwight extended his hand. "Officer…?"

"Taylor. Alex Taylor." The two men shook hands.

"You're the man who saved my A.D.A.'s life today?"

"I guess."

"Why are you still here?" Audrey quickly pressed her fingers to her mouth, embarrassed to hear her reactive thoughts spoken out loud.

His coffee-colored gaze flicked over her face, but he grinned at the unintended slight. "Good to see you again, too."

"I'm sorry. I just… You aren't supposed to be…" Damn. She dropped her hand into a fist at her side. She hated when her words got tangled up in her head like that. Taking a breath to buy herself a moment to articulate her thoughts, she tried again. "I thought you went back to the courthouse to get your truck."

"Already did. I'm parked out front."

Her boss, however, seemed to have no problem with this man making himself at home in her space. "You know Detective Josh Taylor? He's a good friend of mine."

"That'd be Uncle Josh."

"Chief Taylor over in the Fourth Precinct?"

"Mitch is another uncle. I'm Gideon's son."

"Chief investigator at KCFD." Dwight nodded, recognizing the name. "He broke that serial arsonist case a few years back."

Alex's pride was evident in his grin. "Ten years ago. That was the year I met him and Mom. They adopted me."

"If you're a Taylor, then you're the kind of man I'm looking for. You on the clock?"

"Not tonight, sir."

Dwight glanced down at her before making a proposition to Alex. "Feel like volunteering for protection duty with the D.A.'s office?"

"Dwight—" Audrey protested, but these two were already bonding and planning the next few hours of her life for her.

"You want me to drive Audrey home?"

"And stay with her until I can get some kind of official protection detail arranged with the department."

"Yes, sir."

"What do you do with KCPD, Taylor?"

"I'm SWAT, sir."

Dwight touched Audrey's elbow and pulled her forward, as though one man was handing her off to the other. "Then you're in good hands. You focus on the case, and Taylor here will focus on keeping you safe. Now if you'll excuse me, I have a holiday program with my son and a bunch of first graders to get to." Audrey turned in the doorway, determined to make her own opinion heard. But Dwight's gray-green eyes seemed almost pained as he pointed to her cheek. "Be sure to have that looked at." Then he peered beyond her shoulder to Alex. "I'm counting on you."

"My pleasure, sir." Alex's hand settled at the

small of her back and she bristled. The handoff was complete. "I won't let you down."

As soon as they were alone, Audrey shimmied away from the warmth of his hand and stormed around her desk. "'My pleasure,'" she scoffed.

Wasn't the whole point of breaking away from her father's influence so that she'd have the ability to make her own decisions? So that she could have his respect as well as his love? So that he'd see her as a grown-up instead of forever his little missy?

And now, without so much as a consultation regarding her wishes, she had an armed escort driving her home. Either her father would think she couldn't handle herself on her own out in the big bad world and would jump in to make things right, or he'd be so worried that his health would start to decline the way it had when her mother had been ill.

Audrey opened her attaché and pulled out the folders which had gotten knocked around during

the explosion and Alex's saving tackle, straightened the papers inside each one, and neatly
tucked them back into her bag again. Pull.
Straighten. Close. Insert. Maybe she couldn't do
this. Maybe Dwight and her father were right to
worry that she was in over her head. Straighten.
Close. Insert.

"Try not to look so disappointed, counselor.
It's hard on a man's ego."

Alex's teasing voice skittered across her ear-
drums, his tone a calm, patient contrast to her
furious sorting and packing. She shot him an
irritated look as he sauntered around the desk
toward her. "Your ego isn't my concern."

"The D.A.'s right. After everything I've seen
today, you need someone watching your back."

"I don't need a babysitter," she informed him.
"Having you or anyone else dogging my every
move makes it look like I can't do my job. I
studied Demetrius Smith inside and out. I *know*
he has a history of using intimidation tactics to

get what he wants. I'm prepared for that. I won't give him the satisfaction of thinking he's gotten to me." She pointed a file out to the empty offices beyond her door. "Yet after just one day of this trial, my own boss thinks I can't take care of myself. I can't accept that."

Alex caught her hand and pulled the file from her fingers, interrupting her desperate need to maintain control of some aspect of her life.

"How about you accept a recon expert who can make sure all the people around you stay safe?"

"What?" The warmth of his touch was as unsettling as it was unexpected. But her gaze landed on the shredded hem of his sleeve and she couldn't seem to make her fingers pull away from his.

"Maybe you *are* invincible. But the people around you tend to get hurt."

"That's not funny." A quick glance up to his rugged face, which needed a shave and a few hours of sleep, told her the teasing had stopped. Had something else happened during her meeting with Dwight? "I thought your friend said no one in the park got hurt this afternoon—that it was mostly property damage."

"He said no one got seriously hurt."

A fist of guilt squeezed her gut as she took in the bruised and raw knuckles of the hand holding hers. She followed the snagged forearm of his sleeve up to the rip at his elbow. Her gaze moved higher and her pulse quickened. The black knit shirt hugged his biceps and shoulders, stirring some purposely guarded hormones. But her gaze came back to the drops of blood staining his sleeve and his scraped-up knuckles, waking something much deeper. She touched her fingertips to the frayed cotton.

He'd ruined his sweater saving her life. He'd gotten hurt protecting her. This wasn't how today was supposed to happen. She curled her fingers into her palm and raised her gaze to his, discovering just how deep and dark those brown eyes were. She was scared to think he could see that deeply into hers. "Are you all right?"

Alex leaned his hip against the corner of her desk and sat, tugging her half a step closer. Her thigh brushed against his, the soft wool of her skirt catching against his denim jeans and the hard muscle underneath. The shock of heat radiating from the frictive caress surprised her. One little brush and her emotions began to cloud her thinking. "I'm okay," he assured her. "I'm just as tough as I look." He reached up with one finger to brush her hair away from her cheek and tuck it behind her ear. "Have you looked in a mirror lately?"

Audrey jerked up her chin, fighting the instinct to turn her face into the gentle caress of his hand. "So I ruined a pair of panty hose and suffered a few bumps and bruises. I've had worse."

Alex pressed his lips into a tight line. "It could

have been a *lot* worse. The D.A.'s right about a protection detail. Today was just about sending you a message."

The note she'd gotten during the party last night blipped into her mind, along with the creepy attention she'd gotten from Bud Preston. She had the feeling he'd been up to something far more sinister than parking cars. The message that someone meant to terrorize her was perfectly clear. But Alex's argument wasn't any comfort.

"A friend of yours was murdered a month ago. And now a bomb goes off when you've got the press and public hounding your every move. If you won't think about yourself, think about the rest of us. Trip said there were no serious injuries at the park this afternoon, but that might not be the case next time someone comes after you."

"Do you think this is about the Rich Girl murders? Not the Smith trial?"

"I don't know what to think. Yet." He adjusted

his grip, sliding his fingers beneath the sleeve of her jacket. "But how many people have to get hurt before we do figure it out?"

"I didn't think about that. About them. What if he goes after my father? Or hurts a guard or sets off a bigger bomb or…" Frustration, confusion, guilt and fear all fought to find words inside her. But the calloused pad of his thumb, tracing slow circles at the pulse point of her wrist, seemed to short-circuit her usual eloquence. "I don't want anyone to get hurt because of me. But I won't quit this case, Alex. I can't."

"I don't want you to." Tiny bubbles of heat pooled in her blood where he touched her. "Smith doesn't get to win. I won't let him. I don't want you to let him, either."

Strange, how his words of support fueled the warmth seeping through her body. She hadn't realized how badly she needed to hear them. She never expected to feel this urge to turn her cheek against one of those shoulders and have

Alex's strong arms and body wrap around hers. He could keep her safe. He could make her feel.

It wasn't until she saw her own hand, splayed at the middle of his chest, and felt herself leaning in, her legs butting for a more intimate position against his thigh, that she realized where her emotions were leading her. Clearing her throat, Audrey pulled away, breaking all contact with Alex's body. She picked up the file folder with both hands, keeping her fingers occupied and her desires on hold until she could get her thoughts back in order.

"Since I have an early morning in court, we should be going." She stuffed the folder into her attaché, saw there was nothing left to fiddle with on her desk and needlessly reached into the bag to check her phone and wallet and keys. Alex sat there, watching, his dark eyes barely blinking as she angled her chin and laid out her own expectations. "You can walk me to my car in the parking garage and follow me home."

"You're riding with me."

"I'll show you how the security system at home works, and you'll see how safe we are. I'd like to introduce you to my father before you leave, and tell him why you're there."

"I'm staying the night."

"He's probably already seen or heard something about this afternoon on the news."

"Audrey."

"I can call for a driver in the morning—or have a black-and-white follow me into the city."

"You forgot this." Alex slowly straightened beside her, holding up the blood-stained, wrinkled, faded blue bandanna he'd been sitting on.

Heat rushed into Audrey's cheeks and she plucked it from his fingers. It was so soft, still warm from the press of his body. "I didn't mean to keep it so long. I'll get this washed and ironed and returned to you. It was clean this afternoon before…" Right. It was blood-stained.

She stuffed it inside her bag. "I'll buy you a new one."

"Stubborn, I understand. It matches the hair." She turned to get her coat from the stand beside the door, but Alex was there, blocking her path. Grinning. "But I never pictured you as the sentimental type."

When it became clear he wasn't going to move, Audrey tipped her chin to look him in the eye. "I am not sentimental. Don't read anything more into keeping your gift—your old bandanna—than the fact that I just got busy and forgot I had it. I'll replace it. Your sweater, too. And pay for any medical expenses. I suppose I'll have to pay the city to replace that trash can, also."

"Shh." He reached up and traced his fingertips along the line of her jaw.

Audrey shivered and pulled up. "I insist. You probably saved my life. The least I can do is buy you a—"

"I'm not interested in your money," he whispered, capturing the point of her chin between his thumb and fingers. He gave her chin the gentlest of tugs down. "I just don't want to see you hurt again. Not by violence or pressure or loss."

"Stop that." Was that husky gasp her own voice? And what was so damned mesmerizing about the supple articulation of Alex Taylor's lips?

"Stop what?"

Audrey opened her mouth, drew in a breath to speak. The scent of his skin filled her nose, distracting her from her argument. His dark eyes hooded and she watched in perplexed fascination as the distance between them vanished and he closed his mouth over hers.

It was a gentle kiss. An unexpected kiss. A very leisurely, thorough, thought-stopping kiss.

Alex pressed his lips to hers, warming her mouth. He touched his tongue to the bow of her mouth, tasted one corner, then the other. The lightest of stubble rubbed against the swell of her bottom lip, leaving it tender and achy and reaching out to hold on to his when he would have pulled away. His tongue stroked the seam of her lips and they parted to feel the warmth of his breath mingling with hers. She tasted the salt on his skin, the coffee he'd been drinking on his tongue. With a helpless moan, she opened more fully, seeking more, welcoming him.

He slid his fingers along her jawline and tunneled them beneath the hair at her nape. There was nothing connecting them beyond his fingers in her hair and his mouth moving over hers. And heat. Languid, silky, slow-moving heat that flowed from his touch into her skin, seeping through her blood, finding and filling a neglected well of doubt and need and want deep inside her.

Audrey's thoughts were cloudy, her skin feverish with a blush of desire when Alex finally pulled away. She felt his chest rise and fall beneath the clutch of her fingers balled in the front of his sweater. His breath washed over her cheek in a rhythm as deep and unsteady as her own. She saw the lines crinkling beside his beautiful eyes and knew he was smiling.

"Why did…? I can't…" she stuttered.

He brushed his thumb across her lips, sparking and soothing each nerve ending in its wake. "It's okay, Red. I feel this thing between us, too."

Audrey plucked her hand away and curled it against her stomach, but she couldn't come up with a single word to agree with or deny his hushed revelation.

"Nice." He stamped her with a quick peck on the lips, looped her bag over her shoulder and retrieved their coats from the hook beside the door. "I'll have to remember that trick next time I want to get a word in edgewise."

"Trick?" A knee-jerk instinct left Audrey

fuming at the amusement at her expense. Whatever heat had dissipated flooded back into her cheeks. Kissing her into silence? Like she could fall prey to some Neanderthal tactic that short-circuited her poise, rerouted her goals and left her thinking only about him, about them, about the next time he might kiss her.

But she wisely turned her back and let him help her into her coat, keeping her sensitized lips pressed tightly together. She had no position to argue from when the man was only telling the truth.

HE SCRUBBED THE BABY WIPE over his face, cleaning off the last of the black makeup he'd worn with his costume. A satisfied smile looked back from his reflection in the mirror.

Audrey Kline had been scared—he'd read it in the shock that had blanched her skin. She'd been hurt—nothing serious, but enough to know he meant business. She'd been confused by the attack—and maybe that was the most delightful result of all. Confusion and uncertainty had to be particularly frightening for a woman who was used to power and control and having the last word.

Now *he* was the one in control.

He'd seen the way she'd looked at him. He knew her inside and out—what she cared about, what she feared. She was afraid. She was fighting it. But he'd seen that fear. He'd smelled it on her.

She could throw her money and prestige around, and smile her pretty smile. Hell. Even he'd succumbed to it. But no more. She could steal the spotlight and have her pick of men and a career. But if she thought for one minute that she was better than him, that she could overlook him and not regret the slight, that she could keep him from achieving the success that was rightfully his, then she was woefully mistaken.

Audrey Kline had no power over him. No power. Nada. None.

He tossed the soiled cloth into the trash and carefully nestled the rectangular wipe dispenser box against the sink splash. He had to give his toothbrush and razor a nudge so that they lined up parallel to the dispenser, but the calming release he expected didn't come.

He pressed his fingertips to the knot of tension balling at his temple. Why did he always have to fix things? Why couldn't his world fall into place by itself? Now he had to turn his cell phone ninety degrees on the countertop so that it matched the pattern around the sink. The time flashing on the screen annoyed him further. Today had been a complete success, but the momentary balance in his world was already beginning to shift. He was running out of time to savor the memory of Audrey sprawled on the ground beside the sidewalk, bleeding and afraid—clinging to a stranger because she was too damn stubborn to let anyone besides her precious father into her life.

Hmm. That was a possibility. Rupert Kline was a harder target to reach, but he could certainly prove to be Audrey's Achilles' heel.

If he needed a Plan B.

He breathed in deeply, watching his nostrils flare in the mirror—seeing the intelligence and foresight that so many people missed reflected in his eyes. A slow smile crept across his mouth. He had yet to need a Plan B.

He released the breath he held and splashed some soap and water on his face. If he didn't get his butt in gear, he'd be late and he'd miss the opportunity to see the aftereffects of the explosion and threats with his own eyes. And that was a payoff he didn't want to miss.

Reaching for his clothes, he mentally fought to maintain the control that was slipping through his fingers. After dressing quickly, he went back to the mirror to pull on his jacket and smooth out the wrinkles in his lapels and collar. A tug here, a brush there—finally, he was satisfied that he looked the part expected of him. He'd see Audrey soon. Would she be distressed? Angry? Putting on a brave show for her father? It was too much to hope that she'd fall to pieces. Yet. But the opportunity to observe the results of his handiwork was a reward that hurried him out the door and into his vehicle.

He was speeding out of the city toward the posh suburb where the Klines lived like royalty when his phone rang. He read the number, cursed at the annoyance and pulled onto the interstate before answering the call. "What is it now?"

"The blast didn't kill her!"

This was getting tiresome. "It wasn't supposed to."

"This is your idea of a plan? We're the ones

in there with the cops, risking *our* necks. We're the ones they're gonna come talk to—you know that."

"Don't worry."

"Don't worry?" The caller cursed. "We tried to kill that hotshot lawyer today. The cops are gonna come straight to us."

That wasn't his concern. Still, his partners did offer a unique talent for violence and distraction that served his purpose, and he wasn't ready for them to go to jail. So he'd taken care of them. "Do you know how that bomb was put together?"

"No."

"Do you know who I am? Can you give the police my name or describe my face?"

"I can give them this phone number." Although the tone was menacing, it was an empty threat.

"This is a disposable cell—they won't be able to trace it. And since we've never met, you can't identify me." He paused long enough to signal his turn onto the exit ramp. "If you used a stolen car like I suggested and then disposed of it, the police won't be able to put you at the scene of the crime. And if they do, there's no way they can tie the bomb to you. You never touched it—you just happened to be in the wrong place at the wrong time—like your boss claims happened to him. The most they can get you for is throwing fruit at a pretty woman. I've given you plausible deniability."

"You've given me what?"

Idiot. He expelled an impatient breath as he pulled up to a stop light. Then he spelled it out in simple words. "I've taken care of everything. I took out your witness for you. You rattled the assistant D.A. for me. Events have been set into motion. There's no way she can win this case now."

But he'd enjoy watching every humiliating

moment of the end of Audrey Kline's career. He'd revel in it.

Right up until the moment he had to kill her.

Chapter Six

"See?" Audrey said, her tone a mix of high-class attorney and told-you-so bravado. "My father paid a fortune for the best. State-of-the-art. You can only get through the gate if you have a pass card to swipe or you punch in the code—which changes daily."

Alex handed back her security card and waited for the tall wrought-iron gates at the end of her driveway to swing open. Despite the modern additions of technology, this place was like the castle keep out of some damned fairy tale. Tall granite and limestone walls covered in ivy faced the street, and the lights on the other side of those walls illuminated a stand of massive ancient oak trees and a long brick driveway leading up to…well, he couldn't quite make out anything through the skeletal branches beyond a three-story tower and a pair of porch lights. This place might be steeped in old money and architectural history, but it was built for privacy from the outside world, not security. "How many employees and family members have these cards?"

"There's just Dad and me. A cook, housekeeper, groundskeeper—although, they typically use the service entrance in the back."

That was already too many people with unrestricted access to the house.

"When they bring in extra staff, or we have guests, we make different security arrangements."

"By issuing extra cards?"

"Sometimes. Or—"

"—you leave the gate open. Hell." She wasn't

going to make guarding her easy, was she? Alex squeezed the truck's steering wheel in his fist, guessing that another cautionary warning from him would lock Audrey firmly in independent ice princess mode, and rule one for a successful protection operation was to maintain the cooperation of the person he was protecting.

The forbidding rock walls that closed off the grounds from the rest of civilization might explain her desire to take the brisk, open-air walk from the courthouse to her office this afternoon. But the more he saw, the more he realized the sense of security Audrey lived with was false. True, Quinn Gallagher's security designs were the best in Kansas City, maybe even the country, and getting inside wouldn't be easy while the system was engaged. But if a perp ever did get beyond those gates, he'd have free rein to commit whatever crime and wreak whatever terror he wanted without anyone on this side of the walls knowing it before it was too late.

Alex pointed to the rotating cameras and motion sensors at either side of the gate as he drove inside. "Are the guards who handle the codes and equipment on-site?"

Audrey's weary sigh echoed across the cab of his pickup truck. But her posture stayed ramrod straight. She was withdrawing into prickly defensive mode again, a far cry from the soft, needy woman who had melted into his kiss less than an hour ago, and clung to him as if he was an anchor on the streets this afternoon. "Not unless Daddy hires extra security for certain events. Otherwise, the system is monitored at the Gallagher Security offices. We've never had a break-in at the house since it was installed, and the few times trespassers have gotten onto the property, Gallagher had someone here in a matter of minutes."

If a perp was bold enough, desperate enough or crazy enough, it only took a matter of seconds to attack or terrorize or kill. Shaking his head, Alex eyed the wide trunks of the trees lining the long brick driveway that still blocked a clear view of the house as they approached. The Chevy's headlights only emphasized the nooks and shadows where an army of bad guys who meant business could hide.

"The Cosgroves had a Gallagher Security system. Yet somebody got to your friend."

Audrey fingered the red mark staining her collar and, for a moment, those slender shoulders sagged. Alex reached across the seat, feeling like a jerk for having to resort to mentioning something so painful to make his point. But she curled her fingers into her collar and hugged her arms tightly around her, wanting no part of his apology or comfort.

He shifted his hand back to the steering wheel and propped his elbow out the open window. The cool breeze up his sleeve and on his face felt good. The subtle spicy scent off her skin and hair had filled the truck and gotten into his head. He needed the fresh air to remind him that he wasn't some overprotective boyfriend here. He was KCPD. He was SWAT. He was a Taylor. He wasn't chauffeuring Miss Fire and Ice because he wanted to uncover why she kept all that passion locked inside her, or to find out what it took to get those responsive lips and grasping fingers to cling to him again. He was strictly the hired help here, and no amount of fascination with a woman was going to change that. The D.A. had asked him to step up tonight because he was available, and because he knew how to keep someone safe. *So do the job, already.* Alex breathed in, blocking the frustration, curiosity and desire this woman triggered inside him with the scent of damp leaves and the terse words of his commander, Captain Cutler. "All the tech in the world can't replace a set of sharp eyes and surrounding yourself with people you trust."

"And who am I supposed to trust, Alex? You? Just because I let you kiss me—"

"Don't throw all that on me, sweetheart. You were right in there with me."

"So I lost control for a minute. You caught me at a weak moment."

"It was an honest moment." He was surprised at how her words stung. Like he went around taking advantage of vulnerable women. "Maybe your defenses were down, but that doesn't mean those weren't real desires and emotions passing between us."

"Fine." Even silhouetted across the seat from him, he could see the elegant point of that chin angling upward again. "So I...find you attractive. You're different from the men I know."

Good different? Or I've-strayed-to-the-dark-side-once-and-that-kiss-will-never-happen-again different? But she was on a roll now, her expression animated, her articulation sharp.

"And I'm grateful to you for...being there when I needed someone. More than once."

Uh-oh. There was a hesitation in that polished speech, a hitch that cut through his own defensive armor. Audrey might *want* to deny whatever was happening between them, but she wasn't denying that there was already some kind of bond between them.

"That doesn't mean I know you. Or trust you. Not enough to give up the things I do know and put my life in your hands."

"Some people you know better after ten minutes than you do after spending a lifetime with them. I knew my adoptive dad was a man I respected the first day I met him. I knew my mom understood where I came from, and loved me, anyway, the first time she hugged me. My birth parents?" Where was this coming from? He never talked about this crap. He tapped his fist against the truck's window frame and opened up the old wounds, anyway. "Tony Pitsaeli used to beat my mom when he was around. I'd hide in the closet or run away. When she came to, he'd tell her that he loved her. Never did understand that relationship. I tried to stop him one time, and he turned his belt on me. She took to drugs to escape the hell we lived in. I took to the streets. I wasn't even a part of their lives anymore by the time he went to prison."

"Alex."

Audrey's harsh gasp told him that he'd said enough to make his point. He slowed the truck and turned to her. She was facing him now. Her hands were still clasped in that protective hug, but even in the dimness of the dashboard lights he could see the color creeping up her neck. No wonder she fought so hard to guard her feelings—with that beautiful porcelain skin, she wore every emotion front and center for all the world to see. Maybe he ought to be protecting that vulnerability as well as her life.

"Don't feel sorry for me, Red." This time he didn't hesitate to reach across the seat and touch her. He stroked the back of his fingers along her jaw, soothing the heat that colored her velvety skin. "I'm in a good place now. I'm my own man. But I've learned a thing or two about the world that may not be so easy to see from your ivory tower. Tony and Rae Pitsaeli were a part of my life for fifteen years, but I sure as hell didn't trust them. Gideon and Meghan Taylor had my loyalty and trust by the end of the first week they pulled me out of foster care."

He didn't take it personally when she checked the impulse to rub her cheek against his palm.

She leaned in, closed her eyes—but quickly snapped them open and pulled away. "So you're saying that we've known each other for only a month, but that, as annoying and presumptuous as you might be, we've shared enough for me to know I can trust you?"

Alex put both hands firmly on the steering wheel and laughed. "Something like that."

"I'll try. But just so you know, it's when I'm not in control of a situation that I feel the most insecure."

"Trust and control are two different issues. You can't always control a situation." Alex glanced over at her as the line of trees thinned and the driveway began to curve. "But you can always trust me."

With that, she settled back into her corner of the seat, her arms crossed, her gaze straight ahead. He could almost hear the wheels churning inside her head as she pondered his promise—no doubt lining up pro and con lists of arguments as to whether she should believe him or not.

Fine. Let her think. He tensed behind the wheel and went on full alert. As the driveway widened into a three-lane parking area, he could see he had plenty to worry about himself. "Is there a party going on here?"

He pulled into a space behind a white van, one of two parked out front, along with nearly a dozen cars and a dilapidated pickup. Could the

Kline estate serve up any more places for some-one or something unexpected to hide?

"More like the aftermath of one." Alex rolled up his window and shut off the engine while Audrey unhooked her seat belt. "We hosted a fundraiser for a fine arts scholarship in Gretchen Cosgrove's name last night. Clarice Darnell has her crew here packing up—probably while she's flirting with my dad." She nodded toward a red compact. "That's her car."

Alex recognized the Darnell name from the newspaper—not that he ever attended the type of pricey shindigs she put on. But apparently Kansas City's elite couldn't throw a party without Clarice at the helm. There was another niggling familiarity about the event planner's résumé, but Alex couldn't put his finger on it. Instead of playing detective, he'd do better to focus on getting Audrey safely inside. "Let's get in the house so I can familiarize myself with the setup there."

"You're my bodyguard only for tonight."

It could be only for one hour and it wouldn't change his training, or his determination to keep her beautiful, stubborn self safe. "Let's get inside the house."

After climbing out, Alex pulled back the front of his jacket to keep his badge in plain view and his Glock close at hand while he circled the front of the truck. The back of one van was open, but empty. The front door of the house was propped open while the brass lamps on either side were blazing.

By the time he reached the passenger door to hold it open and take her hand to balance her while she stepped from the running board down to the bricks, her skin had returned to a creamy shade of pale, indicating she had her emotions firmly back in check. "Did your grandmother teach you these manners, too?"

Alex grinned. "My commanding officer. He

insists we stick close to the target we're protecting."

"There are more motion detectors and cameras installed around the house itself. With an alarm system we key in ourselves. Do you really think Demetrius Smith and his Broadway Bad Boys are smart enough to get past all the monitors and codes here or at the courthouse?"

Alex locked his truck and placed his hand at the small of Audrey's back, staying close to her side as he guided her through the rows of cars toward the front steps. "Maybe not—a direct, drive-by assault like this afternoon is more their style. But Smith has the money to hire someone who's smart enough to get in here. And you know he has a track record for doing whatever it takes to avoid prison time—witness intimidation, threatening the opposing counsel."

For a moment, she paused. Because of his grim words? Or did the hesitation in her step have something to do with the black Lexus that seemed to catch her attention as they passed it? In either case, she wasn't about to share. Her shoulders came back, her chin went up and Alex had to lengthen his stride to keep even as her heels clicked in a faster staccato up the steps.

He caught Audrey on either side of her waist when she jumped back at the edge of the porch. He felt the subtle tremor in her balance and held on as two workmen in coveralls barreled through the open front door, carrying a long folding table between them.

"Sorry, ma'am," the older of the two men said, pausing. "Didn't see you standing there."

Was Audrey inching back into him? Alex slid his arm around the front of her waist, shutting down his body's instant reaction to her firm bottom pressing against his groin and turning his attention to the man with the toothpick wedged at the corner of his mouth. "Move along, guys," he advised.

Toothpick man winked. "Glad to see you've

got your coat tonight, ma'am. I was worried about you catching a chill last night."

Yep. She was definitely moving closer. Hackles that were more male than cop raised along the back of Alex's neck. "Move. Now."

It was an order.

With a friendly salute, the man with "Bud" embroidered above his front pocket nodded to his partner, and they carried the table on down the steps and loaded it into the back of the open van. While Alex tried to process what had spooked Audrey and why his blood was still pumping with a surge of adrenaline that went far beyond standard alertness, she pushed his arm away and stormed inside the house.

Alex dodged a second pair of men carrying another table outside, and hurried into the marble-tiled foyer behind her. Ah, hell. He'd worked the Plaza downtown on Thanksgiving night when the holiday crowds gathered to watch some official turn on the Christmas lights, and hadn't seen this many comings and goings in a confined space to contend with.

There were four more men, packing linens into laundry bags and tearing down tables in the first two rooms extending off either side of the foyer. Another man, this one wearing glasses and a suit and tie, was carrying a clipboard, jotting down notes and moving from room to room. He halted one man carrying a large silver bowl and pointed him back to a serving table, telling him to pack the bowl into a carrier before loading it. There were two women boxing up glasses and at least two more with cleaning supplies, wiping down furniture and vacuuming rugs.

For a split second, Alex lost sight of Audrey completely as she headed for a carpeted staircase. But he glared a worker out of his path and caught up with her as another man called her name. "Audrey?"

Her knuckles whitened as she squeezed the

railing. But she was smiling as she turned to greet the red-haired man who dashed out of a walnut-framed doorway. "Daddy."

Alex retreated a step as she stretched up on tiptoe to trade a tight hug with her father. The older man framed her face between his hands as he pulled away, carefully studying the mark on Audrey's face, kissing her forehead and then wrapping her in another hug. "Don't you ever scare me like that again, missy. I saw it on the evening news. My God. An explosion?" He pulled away again, a loving reprimand stamped on his ruddy features. "And when you didn't answer your phone? It's a good thing Dwight Powers answered his. He told me what happened outside the courthouse."

She pushed some space between them, resting her hand over her father's heart. "I'm sorry. It wasn't my intention to worry you. I left you a message that said I was okay."

"Uh-huh."

Clearly, Alex wasn't the only man in the room who disagreed with Audrey's idea of "okay." Then he felt himself popping to attention as Audrey's father turned to him and shook his hand.

"And you're the young man who saved her."

Audrey made the introductions. "Daddy, this is Alex Taylor of KCPD. My father, Rupert Kline."

"Good to meet you, sir."

Rupert Kline pumped Alex's hand between both of his. "It's good to meet you. Thank you. And don't tell me that you were just doing your job. Thank you."

Alex extricated his hand from the effusive greeting and glanced over at Audrey's slowly rising chin. Father and daughter shared the same coloring, but they were worlds apart when it came to expressing their feelings. He might have spent some time considering what would cause her to rein it all in, but the trio of other well-wishers joining their circle put him firmly back into protector mode.

"Aud. What a terrible thing."

The tall blond suit who'd claimed owner-ship that night at the Cosgrove murder swept past Rupert Kline and pulled Audrey into a hug. When he bent his head to give her a kiss, Audrey turned to give him her undamaged cheek. Alex could tell Blondie wasn't pleased with the friendly brush-off, and if she hadn't shrugged away his lingering grip, Alex would have answered the need to act buzzing through his veins and twisted the guy's grabby fingers from her arm for her.

"When Rupert told me about those gang-bangers accosting you, I thought I'd lost you, too."

She chided him on a pinched breath. "Don't be so melodramatic. I'm fine. This is Harper Pierce. Jeffrey Beecher. Clarice Darnell."

But there was no shaking of hands.

The dark-haired man with the glasses and clipboard stopped her next. "Audrey?"

Pierce elbowed him back out of the circle. "Can't you see we're having a conversation here, Beecher?"

"Harper," Audrey chided.

Beecher adjusted his glasses on the bridge of his nose, his expression unfazed by Pierce's rudeness. He turned his smile to Audrey. "I just wanted to say that I'm glad you're okay. We've been trying to keep your father busy so that he wouldn't get too worried."

"Thanks, Jeffrey."

"Clarice?" Beecher turned to the slightly plump woman with unnaturally blond hair that was swept up and pinned with silk flowers on the top of her head. "Do you want to talk about the delivery options for the museum event?"

"In a minute." Alex cataloged names and faces and tried to gauge their relationship to Audrey. Family. Friend who didn't understand boundaries. Employees. The fiftyish Clarice had linked her arm through Rupert Kline's. The dart of Audrey's gaze indicated that she'd noted the other woman's connection to her father, but didn't seem to mind. "We're so pleased to see you in one piece, dear."

Jeffrey Beecher tapped the edge of his clipboard. "The vans are nearly full. We need a decision on storage versus delivery tonight."

Clarice shot him a killer glare and curled her fingers more tightly into Rupert's sleeve. So she didn't want to be considered one of the Kline's employees. Was there anyone here who wasn't getting on someone's nerves?

"I thought you were going to handle that," Clarice commented.

"Bud's ready to take the vans to either location. But you're the one who signs the checks, boss."

Audrey's gaze slid over to the handyman with the toothpick and the sudden tension in her mouth made Alex hate the commotion surrounding her here even more.

"Could you two discuss your work someplace else?" Pierce snapped.

Audrey's tone strained to remain polite. "I really do need to get upstairs and change out of these clothes."

Beecher moved over to Clarice to chat directly with her while Harper Pierce swung his attention back to Audrey. "But the Hunts offered to host something for the scholarship fund as well, and I think we should take them up on it. We can make the plans while the event planner is here."

"I told you I couldn't do any more of this until the trial was over. Besides, there's the holi—"

"But it's for Gretchen."

"Bud!" Clarice clapped her hands and Audrey jumped.

The tug at Alex's jacket sleeve was as clear as a cry for help.

Enough. Alex plucked his badge from his belt and held it high in the air. "I need everybody out of here. Now."

He shoved his arm in front of Audrey, blocking anyone else from getting to her.

"Alex—"

She better damn not try to pretend she wasn't overwhelmed by all the chaos here. "If you have a key card to the front gate, it needs to be checked in with me before you leave. I'll be changing the access codes immediately."

"How dare you." Clarice propped her hands on her ample hips. "I have every right to be here."

"We're not finished tearing down," Jeffrey protested.

"All of you. Out." Alex took a good look at Bud Preston's sneering grin and nodded toward the nearest exit before turning to Rupert. "Sir, I'm here to protect your daughter on D.A. Powers's orders. Audrey's my only concern. I need to secure this location and she needs her rest."

Thank God somebody here had his priorities straight. Rupert held up his hands, placating the gathering even as he ushered them toward the door. "Officer Taylor is right. It's been a long, difficult day for Audrey." He caught Clarice by the elbow and turned her with a kiss on the cheek. "Can we finish this tomorrow?"

The platinum blonde wasn't going peacefully. "Of course. But surrender my card? What about your invitation?"

"Not now."

"This will mean paying the crew for over-time," Jeffrey pointed out, using hand signals to get his staff to drop what they were doing and head outside.

Rupert whispered something to Clarice and she smiled. Erasing the affronted look she'd had for Alex, she broke away to come back to Audrey. "Some things are more important than money, Jeffrey." She reached for Audrey, but Alex wasn't budging. "I'm just so glad you weren't seriously hurt." Once she understood that she wasn't getting past Alex's protective arm, Clarice touched her own cheek, indicating Audrey's. "I have a great ointment you can put on that to keep it from scarring."

Witch.

Although the grip on his jacket eased, Audrey was still holding on. "I think a hot shower and some sleep are all I really need. Good night."

Rupert held out his arm and Clarice latched on while they retrieved her purse and he walked her to her car. Audrey's sigh of relief was audible before she turned back up the stairs. But this assault on her patience and composure—feeling every bit like the mob at the courthouse that afternoon—wasn't quite over.

When Harper Pierce's foot hit the first step, Alex was there, his hand at the center of Pierce's chest, pushing him back down to the foyer. "You, too, buddy."

The tall man's blue blood was boiling. "Unlike you, Officer Taylor, I am a friend of the family—a good friend of Audrey's. Why don't you go sit out in your squad car and—"

"Harper, please," Audrey interrupted.

"No. I won't be talked to like this by some—"

"Get out of here, Harper." Audrey Kline might be down, but she was by no means out of fight. Once again, the stubborn redhead surprised Alex when she marched back down the stairs and slid her arm around his waist. "He's with me."

"I understand that the D.A. ordered a protection detail—"

"No, Harper." Audrey turned, the subtle swell of her breast branding Alex's chest as she lightly stroked her fingertips across the stubble of his jaw. His pulse raced beneath his skin, chasing the feel of her deliberate touch on him. She might be playing a game for Pierce's benefit, but the possessive, protective rightness of having Audrey pressed to his side felt real enough, and he slid his arm around her shoulders, completing the embrace. "Alex is with me. He's not leaving."

Pierce eyed the hand cupping Audrey's shoulder before throwing what sounded like an accusation at her. "So you're taking him to the Hunts' New Year's Eve reception?"

"Maybe. If I go."

"I thought we would attend together."

"When did you ask me? Has anyone even received an invitation?"

"Well, I never expected you'd take your boy toy instead."

That's it. Alex had Pierce by the back of his belt and his pretty starched collar and was dragging him across the foyer and out the door before he even got a threat about *suing his ass off* out of his mouth. Pierce was stumbling onto the porch when Alex slammed the door and threw the dead bolt.

Alex turned to face Audrey on the stairs, the sudden emptiness making the house seem even larger than before. He locked on to Audrey's emerald gaze as he strode silently back across the marble floor. She seemed smaller, even more vulnerable than before, framed by the grand staircase. "Your father has the key to get back in, doesn't he?"

Audrey nodded. "And he'll reset the alarm." Her soft smile was worth every curse being hurled at him from outside the door. "Harper *is* a talented attorney. He could take you to court."

"I'm a police officer carrying out my assigned duty. He's got no case against that, does he, counselor?"

"No." Alex halted two steps below her and watched her smile press into a flat line. "I'm going to bed. There are plenty of guest rooms in the east wing. Food in the kitchen—maybe even coffee. Make yourself at home. Good night."

She'd pulled off both shoes and unbuttoned her coat and blazer before she reached the top of the stairs and turned down the west hallway. The coat was sliding off her shoulders when Alex bounded the stairs behind her. By the time she pushed open a door near the end of the corridor, he'd caught up and slipped through the doorway behind her.

"What are you doing?" Weary as she was, there was nothing lagging about the sharpness of that tongue. He noted the length of the pale green sofa beneath the window in the curving tower room and two doors leading into a bathroom and an elegant bedroom of flower patterns and pastels. "Get out of here."

He watched as she tossed her coat and shoes onto the bed and followed him into an equally elegant, though decidedly less flowery office. "You said to make myself at home." He opened a door that led back into the hallway. "Does this lock?"

"Yes." He closed it, locked it. She followed him to the window where he checked the lock and closed the drapes as well as the blinds. "I meant in a guest room."

Back in her bedroom, he checked each window lock and pulled the drapes, ensuring that no curious eyes could even see whether or not the lights were on. "You sleep in here, right?"

"Yes."

"Stay away from the windows. If anyone besides that crowd downstairs gets onto the grounds, I don't want them to be able to identify which rooms are yours." The walk-in closet and bathroom had no exterior exits and were easily secured. But Audrey was with him every step of the way as he learned the layout and identified the access points. A suite of four rooms— the same number of rooms he had in his entire apartment—were a lot easier to defend than the entire house and acreage outside. He returned to the sitting room and tossed his jacket onto the couch. "I can sack out here for the night."

She picked up the leather jacket, stuffed it back into his arms and tried to push him out the door. But her tongue was no match for his strength. "No, you can't. This is my home. These are my rooms, my space."

Which had been violated by at least twenty different people downstairs, and that didn't even take into account pushy reporters and bombs and Broadway Bad Boys. Alex saw the frustration—maybe even desperation—coloring her skin, making the strawberry on her cheek stand out in stark relief. "You expect me to guard you from the blind side of those rock walls and trees a quarter of a mile away?"

She almost said yes. Almost. Either he'd made his point or she'd grown too tired to argue.

Alex again laid his jacket across the couch,

then gently took her by the shoulders and turned her back into the adjoining bedroom. "I won't let Demetrius Smith or his gang or anybody you don't want to see come near you tonight. Get some sleep. Be ready to kick some ass in court tomorrow morning. Close the door if you need some quiet time. Lord knows you deserve it."

Although he could have followed her right over to that queen-size bed, he released her and retreated to his side of the doorway, giving her the distance she wanted—the distance he needed. Something about this woman—everything about her—made him buzz with energy. He wanted when he was around her—he wanted to talk, to discover, to argue, to kiss, to touch, to protect—he probably wanted a lot more than he should.

She was hugging her arms around her waist when she turned to face him. He locked his feet inside his shoes, fighting how much he wanted to take her in his arms and shield the vulnerable beauty that was peeking out beneath her determined exterior. "How do I know you'll stay in there and not invade my privacy?"

"Lock the door if you still don't trust me. I'll knock it down if anything happens and I need to get to you."

Her chin jerked up. She studied him from shoulder to shoulder, noted his gun, his badge, his unblinking eyes. Finally, she resigned herself to the fact that he wasn't going anywhere. Not tonight. She clasped the door in both hands.

"Good night, Alex."

"Good night, Red."

Once she'd closed the door, Alex unhooked his belt and placed his Glock and its holster on the lamp table within arm's reach of the couch. He peeled off his tattered sweater and spread it over the throw pillows he stacked at one end. He turned off the lamp and settled onto the couch, getting accustomed to the sounds of the wind in the trees outside, and Rupert Kline coming back into the house and climbing the stairs. He heard Audrey moving in her bedroom, opening a drawer, crawling into bed.

And as clouds gathered outside and the house fell silent, he noted that, although the door between them was shut, Audrey had never locked it.

AUDREY STARTLED AWAKE at the clap of thunder that punctuated the explosion tearing through her in her nightmare.

Lightning flashed outside her window as she jolted up in bed, her mind racing, her heart thumping against the wall of her chest. She reached over to turn on the lamp beside her, centering herself in the familiarity of her own bedroom.

Seriously, a thunder-snow? While this type of weather wasn't unheard-of in the Midwest, as the seasons fought with each other to change, dumping a mix of rain, sleet and snow while the night sky rumbled overhead, the timing of the violent storm made Audrey wonder if this was still part of her nightmare.

But no, she was alive, she was awake and she was painfully alone.

As her breathing slowed to a healthier rate, she kicked off the covers that had twisted around her hips and tugged down the pant legs of the silk pajamas that had ridden up past her knees. The flashes of the storm peeked through the edges of her drapes, casting strobelike shadows over the Monet hanging on her walls. Matching sparks of adrenaline, remnants of the violent images that had haunted her dreams, coursed through her, making the idea of sleep as appealing as it was now elusive. Her one consolation as she grabbed a pillow and hugged it to her chest was that she must not have cried out or Alex Taylor would be in here already.

She'd seen the look in his eyes earlier—dark like the night, yet filled with such a light that she imagined he could see around corners and deep into her soul. Those eyes were as unsettling as they were handsome, and they'd left her with no doubt that, should he see fit, he'd bust down a door that had survived a fire, a tornado and hooch runners during Prohibition.

It was an idea that was equal parts frightening and reassuring and just a little bit exhilarating.

Why couldn't she have dreamed about that? Alex's hard, compact wrestler's body. That teasing grin. His gentle, drugging kisses. Those eyes.

But no—the rumble of thunder drummed along her spine and she shivered. The flashes of light and shadows creeping through her room transformed into the scattered images from her forgotten dreams. Speeding cars. Cold-eyed stares from a man she knew to be a killer. Grabbing hands. Exploding lights. *Are you scared yet? Do the right thing. Or die doing the wrong one.*

"Stop it." Audrey pulled her knees up and wrapped her whole body around the pillow, finding little comfort. Sitting here, wide awake, trembling in the dark, left her little to do but think.

It had taken forever to fall asleep. She was self-conscious about the man on the other side of her door, obsessing about the trial, remembering the threats, reliving the fear. Audrey looked over at the clock on the table beside her and groaned. Only an hour had passed since she'd last checked the time, shortly after midnight. That didn't bode well for a rested morning. She punched her pillow, lay back down and rolled onto her side. But the intermittent rumble of thunder and her own troubled thoughts kept her from falling back to sleep.

Out of all the craziness she'd gone through since Gretchen's murder, she could count on one hand the number of times she'd felt any real sense of calm or balance in her life. The first time, Alex Taylor had been offering her a hand-kerchief and holding her hand, another… She turned her lips into the cool cotton of her pillow case and remembered how warm and supple and completely seductive Alex's kiss had been.

There'd been one sane voice, one salvation through all of her waking nightmare of the threats and the trial—and he'd been talked down to by her friends and relegated to sleeping on a couch. Shamed by the way Alex had been treated by her guests downstairs, Audrey peeked over to see a dim light shining beneath the crack of her door.

Maybe she wasn't the only one who couldn't sleep tonight.

And maybe the need to offer an apology wasn't the only reason she slipped from beneath the covers and padded across the room.

When she quietly opened the door, Audrey wasn't surprised to see Alex sitting up in the next room.

"Did the storm wake you?" he asked, his voice a hushed echo of the thunder rumbling outside.

"My guilty conscience did. Couldn't you sleep, either?"

"I'm on guard duty, remember?"

The fractured images from her nightmare scattered into the recesses of her mind as something embarrassingly feminine and far too basic pumped into her blood at the sight of his half-naked body. He unfolded himself from the couch, creating ripples of awareness through the sitting room. There was much to appreciate about his sculpted pecs with their dusting of blue-black hair. His stomach was flat, his arms and shoulders heavily muscled. And the most intriguing thing was that, even though he stood only a few inches taller than she, everything about him was supremely masculine and perfectly balanced, from the leather bands on either wrist to the thin stripe of dark hair that disappeared behind the open snap of his jeans.

But she hadn't come out here to give her hormones a rush. She hugged her arms around her middle and rubbed her arms, the unexpected warmth firing inside her creating a chill along the surface of her skin. "I want to apologize for Harper's behavior."

"Why?" He tossed the magazine he'd been reading onto the couch. "You weren't the one throwing out the insults."

"He's not himself. He's still grieving over Gretchen's murder, and he's turned to me as a friend in need."

Alex propped his hands on his hips, refusing to accept her apology. "You're grieving, too. You've got your own problems to deal with. Who's taking care of you?"

"I take care of me." It was a valiant statement, but she wasn't even convincing herself.

"Why did you really come out here?" His eyes were fathomless in the shadows, his voice barely a whisper. Yet everything about Alex's words resonated deep in her bones. "What do you need tonight, Audrey?"

She ran through her list—polite apologies, thank-yous, fear of failing at the trial and letting Demetrius Smith and his lawyer make a mockery of her, fear that others around her would get hurt by her quest, guilt that a friend had died and she'd been too busy to be a very good friend to her at the end. But those dark, all-seeing eyes saw deeper inside. "I want to let down my guard for a few hours. I don't want to be responsible for anyone or anything. I just want to…be taken care of for a little while." The admission ended on half a laugh that just might be masking a few tears. She pressed her fingers to her mouth. "Oh, God, I do sound like a pampered princess, don't I?"

"You sound like an honest woman." He crossed the room with such purpose that Audrey instinctively backed away. But he caught her before she reached the doorway, tugged on her fingers and swung her up into his arms.

"Alex!" She tumbled against heat and strength and found herself not knowing exactly where to put her hands or even if she was pushing away or holding on. His chest hair tickled her palm. His bare skin was hot to the touch. A muscle flexed when she touched him there. He grinned when she touched him there. "Alex?"

"Shh. Around my neck is just fine."

She lightly wound her arms around his neck and held on as he carried her into her bedroom. Although certain traitorous parts of her had one idea in mind, Alex was taking her at her word, giving her what she'd asked for, what she needed. He laid her on the bed and tucked the covers up around her chin. After a gentle press of his fingertip to her lips, he left the room. Audrey had pushed herself up onto her elbows, wondering at his game, when he returned with his gun and badge. The edge of her bed sank beneath his weight as he leaned over to place his ID and weapon within easy reach.

But before he turned off the light, she saw the puckers of pale circular scars on the back of his right shoulder, like a spider's web standing out in harsh contrast against his olive skin. With her stomach clenching in knots of compassion, she reached up and brushed her fingers across the palm-size wound.

His skin jumped beneath her touch. And then Alex was turning, plucking her hand away and swinging his legs up on top of the covers beside her. "Easy, Red. You asked for comfort, and I'm doing my damnedest to be a good boy here."

"What happened to you?"

"Nothing too dramatic—laser surgery." He scooted down onto the pillows and rolled onto his side to face her. "I had a tattoo removed."

"A good-size one from the look of it. Did it hurt?"

"Not as much as when an old friend tried to cut it off me."

Audrey hissed at the horrid idea of the pain he must have suffered. She laid her fingers against his cheek, cupping his stubbled jaw. "Alex…"

He covered her hand with his. "It was a gang tat, Audrey. Westside Warriors. I may be the best qualified cop in KCPD to protect you against Smith. Because I grew up in a gang, too."

He didn't seem surprised when she freed her hand to clutch the sheet and comforter together at her chest between them. Maybe he thought she was judging him, but she was just…stunned. "Did you ever…?"

"Get into trouble?" He rolled onto his back and stared at the ceiling. "Yeah. Not anything I'm proud of. All juvie stuff. I finally got out the year before the Taylors adopted me. They made me want to stay out."

"Don't gangs have some kind of violent…reverse initiation…if a member wants to leave?"

"Yeah."

He didn't elaborate and his stark response left Audrey imagining all kinds of horrible things—like peeling off a tattoo with a knife—and crawling out from under the covers to hug him tightly around his shoulders.

After a moment's hesitation, he folded his arms around her and pulled her squarely on top of him, holding her close for several timeless minutes. He buried his nose in her hair and breathed deeply. Audrey rode the rise and fall of his chest, settling more deeply, more intimately against him with every exhale.

But as his hands slid down toward her bottom, he muttered a curse and pushed her away. "You play hell with my best intentions, counselor."

Fine. Keep it friendly. Audrey tried to give him his space. But she didn't get far across the bed before he snaked his arm around her waist and pulled her back into the sheltering curve of his body, as though he, too, had a few needs that could only be assuaged by the closeness of another human being. He drew gentle, mindless circles across her belly as he spooned behind her, warming the silk and soothing something tight and needy deeper inside. "The point is, I know how Smith thinks. I know how a gang works. I know just how tough and ruthless they can be."

So he could be that tough and ruthless, too.

"Does that scare you?" he whispered against her ear.

Audrey laid her hand over his, lacing their fingers together to still the errant caresses. "Having a former juvenile delinquent in bed with the assistant district attorney?"

His chuckle was a warm balm against her skin. "A headline like that couldn't be good for your reputation. A glory-seeker like Lassen would love to print that story."

"I only worry about headlines if they're a lie or they hurt my father."

"You're very protective of him."

"He's all I've got. I want him to know that I can take care of myself out in the world—that he doesn't always have to worry about me. When my mom was dying of cancer, the worries he had ate him up. They aggravated his heart condition."

"That explains a lot about your need to be independent. Striking out on your own and creating your individual success is your way of taking care of him."

"Yeah." He got it. She wasn't sure if that understanding surprised her or not. Alex Taylor seemed to intuit more about her than she even knew herself sometimes. It should have been a disquieting realization to know that someone had gotten so deep into her head. Instead, her body relaxed and she snuggled into the wall of heat at her back. "You're not exactly who I thought you'd be, Alex."

"I'm a different class of people than Pierce and your society friends, hmm?"

She shook her head. This wasn't about social standing. "You're more complex. When I expected you to be an ass, you gave me your handkerchief and stood up for me."

"That's Grandma's training."

She squeezed his hand at her waist and smiled. "I hear such love and unabashed gratitude every time you speak of your family. I never expected that, either. You fight with me—"

"They're discussions, Red."

"—yet you stand beside me when I need a friend." Or lie beside her. A tremor of awareness that had nothing to do with comfort and everything to do with sexual hunger rippled along every inch of her skin. "You're a little hard for me to figure out."

He misread her shiver as a sign she was feeling chilled, and tucked her beneath the covers again. He stretched out on top of the comforter and pulled her into his arms, facing him. "Oh, and that's eatin' you up inside, is it?"

She gave his shoulder a playful swat, followed almost immediately by an unexpected yawn. "Hard, I said, but not impossible. I won't quit trying."

Maybe he was feeling the same sexual tension, but he was determined to give her what she'd asked for. He traced relaxing lines up and down her back and continued the quiet conversation. "You're not what I expected, either."

"Daddy's society princess? That's one of the reasons I went to work for Dwight Powers—I want to prove I'm not that stereotype."

"Trust me, Red, you are too unique to fit into any stereotype I know of."

That comment gave her pause. "You know, that may well be the most meaningful compliment any man has ever given me."

"Who said it was a compliment?"

She giggled against the fragrant warmth of his skin. But his strong arms and abundant heat and quiet conversation were working. Her eyelids had lead weights on them and it was getting harder and harder to focus. She nestled into the pillow of his shoulder with her hand resting at the middle of his chest. "Is there anything else you like about me, Alex?"

She felt his lips in her hair, felt the absolute security of his arms around her. He was taking care of her. In the tenderest way possible, he was giving her exactly what she needed.

"The list is too long to get into tonight. You need your sleep, and so do I."

Audrey wasn't sure when the darkness finally claimed her and she fell asleep. But she knew she wasn't alone. She was in a place where the nightmares couldn't reach her. She was calm, centered, secure in her dreams.

And for the first time in a long while, she believed that everything in her life might just turn out all right.

Chapter Seven

Audrey cracked one eye open as a narrow ribbon of light fell across her face. She put up her hand, wanting no part of pictures and reporters intruding on her blissful slumber this morning.

Slumber? Morning?

She rolled over to a cold spot and shivered. Both eyes snapped open. The bright line of light was peeking through the gap between her drapes. The storm had passed, the alarm clock was beeping and she was alone.

Alone.

She threw back the covers and scrambled out of bed. "Alex?"

The intimacy of holding each other through the night had passed. The doors were closed, the room was silent, his gun and badge were gone. How dare he? Not even a goodbye? He'd done his duty by her—he'd talked and shared and aroused and comforted and now he was gone? Or had something happened? Had his team been called out on a dangerous assignment? Had someone gotten onto the estate, after all? She went through confusion, anger, hurt and, finally, concern, as she ran to the sitting-room door and pulled it open.

"Alex!" She screamed when she saw the giant perched on the end of her couch and jumped back to cling to the door frame. "Who are you—? Where—?"

"Trip Jones, ma'am. Remember me from yesterday in the park? I'm a friend of Alex's from SWAT Team One. Didn't mean to startle you."

Now she saw the gun at his hip, the insulated SWAT jacket draped over the back of the couch. He set down his book and stood. And stood. And stood while she shrank back another step and estimated the distance to the hallway.

"Shrimp asked me to come over and keep an eye on things while he gets cleaned up."

Shrimp? She swiveled her head to the sound of running water and the door to the bathroom swinging open.

"Audrey!" Alex ran straight toward her, clutching a towel around his waist, dripping on her rug. With a muttered curse, he stopped and turned to the big man with the light brown hair. "You couldn't have announced yourself?"

"I didn't realize you hadn't told her that we were here. We were just getting acquainted."

"Wait a minute, *we?*" There were more armed police officers lurking around the house?

"Shrimp called for reinforcements." Trip grinned, never retreating one step from Alex's advance. "Now I can see why. You're sportin' a real tough-guy look there. Where are you hiding your gun?"

"You don't want to know." Alex slicked his fingers through his wet hair and glanced back at the bathroom. "Why don't you go outside and check the grounds?"

"Holden and Sarge are already on that. Captain Cutler is on the phone with Quinn Gallagher's office, tracking down the security logs to find out everyone who's come and gone from the estate over the past month or so." He shrugged his black jacket onto his broad shoulders. "I called your brother like you asked. He's got his dog here to see if he can pick up any trace of intruders on the grounds."

"There's a dog?"

"K-9 unit, ma'am." Trip turned his warm hazel eyes to her before pulling a black KCPD ball cap over his super-short, military-cut hair. "Although I don't know if he'll be able to pick up much after all that sleet and snow we had last night."

With one hand holding tight to the towel that rode atop his hips, Alex gestured to the hallway door. "Why don't you track down Pike and see how he and Hans are doing?"

"Pike's the brother, Hans is the dog," Trip clarified, easily looking over Alex's shoulder to her before opening the door.

Alex's irritation was as evident as Trip's amusement as he shooed the replacement babysitter out. "I've got this covered in here, big guy. Go find the dog."

"You ain't got much covered." The door was closing in his face as Trip added, "Nice to see you again, ma'am."

Alex ducked into the bathroom to turn off the water and scrub a towel over his short, curling hair. He draped the second towel around his neck and apologized. "Sorry about that. When I called for backup this morning so I could get a couple hours of hard sleep, I didn't think my entire team would show up. You were zonked, so I thought I'd be done before you woke to warn you about the shift change."

Now that she recognized Trip Jones and understood why he was here, she remembered something Alex had said to her outside the courthouse yesterday. Yes, she'd been startled, but he had nothing to apologize for. She grabbed the ends of the towel hanging over his chest and tugged him closer. "Your team is here to back you up because you need them. We need them."

She tugged a little harder and angled his face down to hers to kiss him. His skin was steamy from the shower, his face clean-shaven and smooth. And his lips were just as warm and divine and wonderful as she remembered as he tunneled his fingers into her hair and deepened her *thank you* into a taste of a passionate *good morning.* Audrey curled her toes into the carpet, still holding on to the towel, as she forced herself to pull away.

"Thanks for last night. I guess I needed a little backup myself. You were right about me needing to realize that." She tickled her palm over the curls of hair on his chest. "But the reality of today is I have to return to the courthouse and face off against Cade Shipley and his client."

"Wait a minute. Rewind. I was right?" He slid his hands to the small of her back and pulled her flush against him, smiling against her mouth before he reclaimed it. "I have a feeling that's not something I'm going to hear too often."

Audrey squealed a token protest as the water from his wet skin soaked through her pajamas. It was like standing skin-to-skin, softness to hardness, need to need. Her pulse caught fire. Her nipples pearled beneath the friction of his chest moving against hers, shooting little tendrils of heat curling down inside her. Audrey wound her arms around his neck and pulled herself up on tiptoe, aligning her hips with his, recapturing the closeness they'd shared through the night, intensifying it.

Alex moaned deep in his throat and tore his mouth from hers a split second before the door opened and Trip walked back in. "Sorry. Don't mind the elephant in the room. Forgot my book. By the way, you aren't the only company here this morning. A Miss Darnell? Mr. Kline spoke to Captain Cutler and we cleared her. Otherwise, no one has been here except the paperboy and the morning staff. Just wanted you to know that some of us around here are doing our job, shrimp." He tipped his hat to Audrey and winked at Alex. "You two carry on."

"Get out of here!" Alex ordered.

Audrey landed flat on her feet as Alex released her and whirled around. The wad of towel that had been around his neck hit the closing door as Trip grinned all the way out.

She curled her arms around her waist, setting

up a definite barrier as Alex reached for her to resume the kiss. His gaze narrowed and he settled for rubbing his hands up and down the silk on her arms. "Audrey?"

She backed away a step. She hadn't heard the knock on the door, or whatever had alerted him to Trip's return. He'd been on guard, as usual—aware of everything going on around him. He hadn't forgotten about the threats and his duty, while for the past few moments she'd forgotten about everything except getting that towel off his hips and getting even closer.

She'd forgotten about her duty. To the people of Kansas City.

"Don't be so hard on him." The interruption gave her the moment she needed to get her head screwed on straight. Burying those impulsive urges made her realize a bit of modesty was in order. She went to the door and picked up the towel to cover her now see-through pajamas. "I think the big guy's funny."

"Don't encourage him. *I'm* the guy on the team who gets picked on."

"He probably wasn't expecting us to move so fast into that…" Achy, raw, foolishly wanting to tumble back into bed and share the ultimate closeness feeling that was still reeling through her veins. "I'm sure he wasn't expecting…that."

"Apparently, you weren't, either."

Had she ever seen such an unreadable expression on Alex's face? "I'm sorry."

"Don't." He strode back into the bathroom and collected his jeans from the night before and a gym bag that Trip must have brought him. He tossed them onto the couch, pulled out a pair of black boxer-briefs, boldly dropped his towel and started dressing in front of her. Audrey shielded her eyes from that taut, head-to-toe physique and turned her head. "Don't apologize for acting on what you feel. Trust your gut. Don't overanalyze it and talk yourself out of what you want." He shook out a crisp pair of jeans and stepped into them. Audrey lowered her hand and faced him, knowing he was looking her way. "I don't know what the problem is that you have with us, Red—if it's where I come from, or if you're like Pierce and think I'm just the hired help—"

"No."

"—or if you just can't accept the idea that sometimes things happen quickly between people." He left his jeans unfastened around his hips and crossed the room to her. "We fit, Audrey. You and me, like no other woman I've known before. I don't question it. I don't need time to weigh the whys or why nots, I just accept it."

"How do you know that?"

"I don't. I'm trusting my gut instincts. I feel something for you, you feel something for me. Why is that such a bad thing for you?"

Audrey hugged the towel more tightly in her arms. Alex Taylor's omniscient eyes really could see deep down inside her. No, she hadn't been expecting the intensity of her relationship with Alex to move so quickly. She hadn't been expecting any kind of relationship, period. She was a career woman with a life plan. Falling in love with him wasn't supposed to be on the agenda.

Falling in love?

Oh, Lord. Audrey pulled up the towel to her cheeks to hide the confusion and dismay and fear that his uncanny intuition about her was right on the money.

She did the cowardly thing and headed for the bathroom, plugging in her curling iron and retrieving her hair dryer, desperately needing to sort things out and regain some semblance of control over her life before continuing this conversation. "I have to be in court by 9:00 a.m."

An unexpected hand cupped the back of her neck and turned her. Alex stamped her mouth with a hard kiss and quickly released her. But those dark brown eyes ensnared her with something else. He wouldn't let her be a coward. "You think about it, Red—because I know you like to think. You think about giving us a chance, and I'll be with you all the way. I'll go as fast or slow as you like. But if you decide you just can't let yourself feel what you feel, do me the courtesy of letting me know, okay?"

Were those tears stinging her eyes? "I don't want to make a mistake. I don't want to hurt you."

"I know." He pulled the towel from her hands and dabbed at her eyes. "Maybe better than you do. But I'm worried that you're the one who'll really feel it if you don't give us a chance. Just think about it."

Yes. She definitely needed to think. No matter what karmic wisdom Alex shared about knowing his feelings for people so quickly, this was definitely moving a little fast for her—this needing, this wanting. Her life was changing too fast for her to process. Had she missed

something more than companionship develop-
ing between her father and Clarice? And it was
more than a little scary to think how quickly
she was losing control of the professional relationship she should be maintaining with Alex.
Right now, she needed to backtrack away from
this crazy passion and emotional intimacy and
return to A.D.A.-bodyguard mode for a while.
She pushed him out the bathroom door with a
shaky smile. "Work, Alex. We both have work
to do. I'll have to deal with this—with us—
later."

Alex's scent only intensified in the steamy
room when she closed the door. But she couldn't
be distracted by that right now. She shouldn't
remember how secure she'd felt falling asleep
in his embrace or how hurt she'd been thinking
that he'd left her during the night. She couldn't
think about kissing him and wanting him and
feeling terrifyingly out of her comfort zone and

perfectly in place each time he took her in his arms. Not right now.

Audrey stepped into the shower, turned her face into the spray and let the pelting warmth of the water cleanse the distracting thoughts from her head. By the time she was drying her hair and putting on her makeup, she had the disturbing emotions triggered by Alex Taylor firmly under control. She was rejuvenated, reenergized and ready to take on whatever Judge Shanks, Cade Shipley and his menace-to-society client had to throw at her today.

She was buttoning her brown cashmere blazer over its matching skirt and coming down the stairs to grab a cup of coffee and a muffin when she heard the clatter of silverware on a plate and the sounds of distress coming from her father's office.

"Oh, my God."

Her father's voice.

"What are they doing to her? My little girl."

His pinched, gasping voice turned Audrey's walk into a run. "Daddy!"

"Mr. Kline!" the family cook, Mrs. Puente, called.

"Rupert? Oh, dear," Clarice said.

"Don't let her see this," Rupert demanded.

"Daddy? Alex!" she called to the trio of men and a big German shepherd huddled in a terse conversation just inside the front door.

Audrey dashed through the arched walnut door to find Mrs. Puente and Clarice Darnell hovering over her father in the leather chair behind his desk, trying to give him a glass of water and unbutton his shirt. Rupert Kline's narrowed gaze landed right on her as he clutched at his chest.

Heart attack.

"Daddy!" Audrey dashed to his side.

"It's okay, missy." He tried to smile. "Just a flutter. It'll kick back…into rhythm…in a minute."

She pulled the newspaper from his fist, focusing on his face.

"No!" Rupert wheezed.

She ignored him and tossed it onto the desk, snapping out the orders the doctors had trained her to do. "We need to stretch him out on the floor. Mrs. Puente, get the bottle of aspirin and a blanket. Clarice, call 9-1-1."

"Already done." Alex's voice was right behind her. He and Trip blew past her and lifted her father from his chair, nudging aside Clarice, who was still trying to unhook buttons. Audrey didn't have time to consider the implications of having the platinum blonde spending the night with her father. Alex thrust the phone into her hand. "I told Dispatch the address, you give them the details."

Whatever had happened between them upstairs, thank God, had been thrust aside to concentrate on her father. Alex and Trip were working like a smooth-running machine, asking her father questions and checking his pulse. Grateful for the help, Audrey turned her attention to the 9-1-1 dispatcher on the phone. "Rupert Kline. Yes, he wears a pacemaker. Dr. Trecha is his specialist."

Rosie Puente huddled against the floor-to-ceiling bookshelves, clasping her hands together in prayer. Tears filled her eyes. "I didn't mean to do this. I served him his egg whites and soy bacon and toast, and brought him his paper, just like I do every other morning of the week. And then he grabbed his chest. I didn't mean—"

"Get the aspirin, Rosie. You didn't do anything wrong." Audrey squeezed Mrs. Puente's hands and gave her a slight shake. There was no blame here, she just needed action. "Go." She turned her attention back to the dispatcher on the phone. "We're getting him an aspirin now."

Three more officers, including the sergeant who'd driven the pickup away from the courthouse yesterday, appeared. The oldest man of the group—clearly the one in charge—with dark salt-and-pepper hair, spoke in hushed tones. A tall blond man introduced himself to Clarice as Holden Kincaid and drew the older woman out of the room. Sergeant Delgado jogged out of the room after them, making a call on his own cell phone.

She completed her call to the 9-1-1 operator and knelt at her father's side next to Alex. She smoothed his silvery red hair away from the perspiration dotting his forehead. "It'll be okay, Daddy. The ambulance is on its way."

"It's just a palpitation, missy." He tapped his chest. "That's what the hardware's for. I'll be all right."

Sergeant Delgado came back in with a portable oxygen tank and mask. He handed it off to Trip. "We need to get this on you, sir."

"Just breathe, Daddy." Audrey handed the phone back to Alex, and didn't try to pretend she wasn't grateful for the quick squeeze of her fingers before he slipped the cell into his pocket.

She watched him press those same fingers to her father's thigh, checking his femoral pulse. The germ of a memory, the seed of something crucial to the Smith case she'd overlooked whispered through her mind. She murmured the thought out loud. "He was shot in the leg."

"Red?"

"Calvin Chambers was shot in the chest *and* the leg. I think I just figured out how to win the trial. Since Plan A didn't work, and Plan B is... Never mind." She shook off the idea and focused on the most important issue at hand. "How is he?"

"We've just got basic medic training, but I don't think it's a full-on heart attack. Something must have given him a shock."

"He's still going to the hospital," Audrey insisted.

"I know, Red. I want a professional to check

him out, too." Alex looked back down to her father. "Mr. Kline, can you tell me when this started?"

Rupert seemed to be breathing a little easier with the oxygen mask over his mouth and nose, but he was still alarmingly pale. "Reading that paper." He raised up slightly and grabbed hold of Alex's sleeve. "Don't let them hurt her. You keep her safe."

"Shh. Relax, sir." He eased her father back to the floor. "I'm not going anywhere."

Audrey smoothed her father's hair again and bent down to kiss his forehead, hiding her fear behind a smile. "Hang in there. Don't worry about me—I'm all grown up, remember?"

Rosie Puente huffed into the study, and they covered Rupert with a blanket and helped him swallow one of the aspirins. Within a matter of minutes, the real EMTs were at the house, rolling out her protesting father on a gurney, and assuring her that his heart rate was returning to normal and that the doctor would meet them at the hospital to conduct a thorough check of the patient.

Clarice had a hold of her father's hand and was hurrying alongside the gurney. "I'm so sorry, Rupert. Do you want to reschedule?"

When the EMTs paused at the front door, Audrey glared Clarice away from her father and took his hand instead.

Clarice puffed up, her expression changing from concern to self-defense. "He invited me to breakfast."

Her father's fingers tightened around hers and he pulled the oxygen mask away from his face to give her a wry smile. "You're the one who encouraged me to start dating."

That she had. She'd even suggested Clarice as a candidate. So her campaign to prove to her father that she was a mature adult had just taken a serious setback. Was it because she subconsciously suspected Clarice Darnell was a gold digger? She herself had worked with her on several occasions, and had observed nothing but professional results. Or had she just seen another woman taking her place at her father's side and succumbed to a stab of jealousy? Emotions, right. She glanced over at Alex at the foot of the gurney then quickly turned away from his knowing gaze to replace the mask over Rupert's nose and mouth. "I'm sorry, Clarice." She straightened and faced the buxom woman. "You're welcome to join us at the hospital."

"No." Rupert snatched her hand again. "You have court this morning, and I know you just had a brainstorm that would do the Kline name proud. This trip to the hospital is just a precaution. You can come see me afterward."

"I'll call Judge Shanks. He'll understand an emergency and will grant me the delay."

"Absolutely not." Rupert Kline's killer-in-the-courtroom glare hardened his expression for a moment. "You have a job to do. You're my daughter. If this is what you want, you go get them."

"Daddy—"

"I'm trying to do the right thing here, missy." Fatigue and love softened his face with a paternal smile. "They brought this battle to our home, not once, but twice now. And as much as I want to protect you…" He took the deepest breath he had in the last twenty minutes. "Maybe it's time I handed over the reins and let you do your own fighting. If I was trying this case, I'd do everything in my power to make sure Smith and his thugs didn't win."

He believed in her. As much as he wanted to pamper and protect her, the great Rupert Kline believed she could win this case. Humbled and inspired and deeply grateful for his confidence in her, Audrey leaned down to kiss his cheek. "I'll get him, Daddy."

He winked at her before angling his gaze at

Alex. "I'm counting on you, too, son. You watch her back."

"We need to go, ma'am," the EMT interjected.

Audrey nodded and stepped away. "Do you mind staying with him until I can get there, Clarice?"

"I'll take good care of him, hon."

"I love you, Daddy."

They were already wheeling him out the door. "Love you, too."

Once the ambulance pulled away, with an off-duty police escort, Alex shut and bolted the door. "What did Rupert mean, the battle has been here twice?"

Audrey marched into her father's office where Mrs. Puente had started to clear the tray from his desk. She thanked the cook and sent her off to the kitchen to take a break. Then Audrey went to her father's chair and picked up the newspaper. She frowned. "This isn't the *Journal.* Where did this scandal rag come from?"

She opened it to the second-page photo of her and Alex sprawled on the sidewalk in the middle of the debris field from the exploded trash can. There was tomato on her collar and a bloody mark on her cheek. Her knees nearly buckled. Her father had seen this?

Even more disturbing than the *Attack on A.D.A.* headline was the message drawn across the photo in black magic marker. *He can't save you from the inevitable, bitch!* Audrey felt the same sense of violation and fear as she'd felt yesterday at the park. But she curled her toes inside her pumps and stood tall as she handed the paper across the desk. "This isn't the first threat I've received."

Alex read the words and swore at the noose drawn around her neck. "This is Steve Lassen's work. Damn opportunist."

"The picture and article are his, at least. That doesn't mean he added the message."

Alex set down the paper and pushed it away

as though the sight of it made him physically ill. "And you've gotten other crap like this? That might explain what Pike and his dog found outside."

A chill crept down her spine. "What's that?"

"A set of footprints in the slushy leaves out in your front yard forest, along with a handful of small branches that have been sliced off with some kind of knife."

"The groundskeeper wouldn't trim the trees until all the leaves are gone."

"And he wouldn't hack at it with a knife. Somebody's been here, watching you. Somebody who didn't want to be seen." He unlocked the holster on his belt and pulled out his gun. With a series of precise movements, he dumped the magazine, slammed it into place again, checked the sights and returned it to the back of his belt as if he was expecting a gunfight. *Not ill. Pissed off. Maybe too angry to feel.* Alex needed to *do.* "The D.A. wants me here. Your father wants me here. What about you?"

She met those unblinking dark eyes across the desk. She was ready to take action, too. "Have one of your buddies call the crime lab. See if they can get knife marks off those branches. Hopefully, the storm hasn't degraded the footprints too much. Dust this paper for prints. Make sure they take Clarice's."

"To eliminate her as a suspect?"

Maybe. She didn't see how her father's new girlfriend could possibly have a connection to Demetrius Smith, but Audrey was about facts, not taking chances. "This is a morning edition. Somebody had to bring it in here after you cleared the house last night."

"The Bad Boys could have cornered the paperboy and forced him to deliver it for them. They could have…waylaid him and made the delivery themselves." Forced? Waylaid? Was he speaking from experience? "Sergeant Delgado has already called the lab. Do you know the kid's name?"

Audrey's stomach turned at the idea of another innocent being harmed by the Broadway Bad Boys in their effort to get to her. "Mrs. Puente does."

"I'll have Sarge talk to her and get the info." Alex propped his hands at his waist and re-phrased his question. "What do you want *me* to do?"

"Take me to the courthouse."

Chapter Eight

"Mac Taylor is the day shift commander of the KCPD crime lab, with twenty years of experience in the field. I think he knows what he's talking about." Audrey paced in front of the judge's bench, pointing to the man on the witness stand.

"Objection overruled. I don't think we need to debate the experience of this witness, Mr. Shipley, so sit down." Judge Shanks paused to take a sip of what had to be room-temp coffee by now. He might look tired, but there was no mistaking the pinpoint reprimand in his eyes. "But watch the sarcasm, Miss Kline."

Audrey thanked him with a deferential nod and turned her attention back to the forensic scientist with a scarred face, a blind eye and glasses, who'd remained completely cool and unflustered by Cade Shipley's groundless attack on his skills and the way he ran his office. "Mr. Taylor, back to my previous question. You found no trace of GPR—gun powder residue—on the clothes the defendant, Mr. Smith, was wearing when he was arrested."

"None."

She ignored Cade Shipley's snicker. Did he really think she was foolish enough to pursue this line of questioning if she thought it would prove his client's innocence? "But you said the jacket he was wearing had no bullet hole in it."

Mac Taylor leaned forward to speak directly into the microphone. "Correct. The jacket had his blood on it. Part of the zipper had been broken and ripped out, as though it had gotten caught on something, or he'd gotten frustrated with it when he was putting it on."

"Relevance, your honor?" Shipley protested. "It's after four o'clock and I'm interested in eating dinner sometime tonight."

Audrey bit down on what she thought Shipley could do with his dinner if he kept on interrupting her. She thought it a wiser move to smile at Judge Shanks. "I have a point to make, Your Honor, I promise."

"Then get to it."

She returned to the witness. "So there was no bullet hole in the jacket Demetrius Smith was wearing, yet Mr. Smith's medical records clearly show that he'd been shot in the arm. What conclusion did your lab reach, based on that evidence?"

"That Smith wasn't wearing that jacket when he was shot."

"Now Captain Cutler of the responding SWAT team on the scene has already testified that they stormed the house within a minute of hearing Mr. Smith yelling that he'd been shot and wanted to surrender." She looked out into the gallery watching the trial, reminding the jury of the tall, salt-and-pepper-haired man in his black KCPD SWAT uniform who'd been on the stand earlier. Her gaze skimmed over Alex, sitting beside him. It shouldn't give her that little rush of confidence that he was out there supporting her, protecting her. But those dark eyes watching her did make her think that she could do this. She brought her gaze back to Mac Taylor's sighted eye. "Your lab also processed a jacket worn by another suspect at the scene, Tyrell Sampson. Would you tell the court what you found on Mr. Sampson's jacket?"

Mac nodded. "A bullet hole in the right sleeve. Blood. GPR on the right cuff. And traces of gun oil with minute metal filings that match the gun registered to Demetrius Smith."

"The gun that killed Calvin Chambers?"

"Yes."

"Had Mr. Sampson been shot?"

"Not according to the police report."

From the corner of her eye, Audrey saw Demetrius lean over and whisper something to his attorney. Seconds later, Cade Shipley was on his feet again. "Your Honor, if you recall, in that same police report, the interview with Tyrell Sampson stated that he was already in the system as the victim of a gunshot wound. An accident with a friend who was cleaning his gun, I believe."

Judge Shanks scratched at his curly black beard and sighed into his hand. "So noted. Miss Kline? Your point?"

Audrey cleared her throat to keep from smiling. *Keep going, Shipley. Help me win this case.*

She wrapped her fingers around the railing in front of the witness box and asked a simple question. "Was the blood on Tyrell Sampson's jacket his?"

"No. It was Demetrius Smith's."

Audrey let the grumbling through the court-room gallery subside before she spoke again. "So is it feasible to assume that Demetrius Smith changed jackets with Mr. Sampson in the minute between him being shot and being hand-cuffed by SWAT?"

"A quick-change artist could do it, yes."

Cade Shipley quickly objected. "Your Honor. Speculation."

"Withdrawn." Audrey quickly responded before looking up at Judge Shanks. "I have no further questions for this witness, Your Honor."

"Thank you, Mr. Taylor. You're dismissed."

Audrey returned to her seat, stealing a sly look at the jury as she walked by. She could see by their reactions that she'd successfully put the possibility into their minds that Demetrius had indeed shot and killed Calvin Chambers, and then switched the jacket that held the incriminating evidence as soon as he realized he was going to be captured.

It wasn't a fact she could win a case on. But if she could find one Broadway Bad Boy who'd been on the scene to say he'd seen Demetrius switch jackets, then she didn't need to put the gun in his hand. The forensic evidence would put it there for her.

"All rise."

Audrey checked her watch as the courtroom was dismissed. If the fates were with her, she could wrap up a conviction in a matter of days rather than dragging this out over the holidays or settling for reduced charges against Smith. Alex had put in a call to his uncle Josh, one of the detectives working the Chambers shooting, and he and his partner were rounding up Tyrell Sampson for her to reinterview before the end of the day. Maybe she couldn't get him to state that he saw Demetrius fire the kill shot, but she might be able to get him to say something about changing clothes—unless he wanted to say the jacket with all the evidence was his, and take the rap for killing Calvin Chambers himself.

She tucked her notes into her attaché bag and looped it over her shoulder.

If the fates were…

When she turned to leave the prosecution table, Demetrius Smith was looking right at her. Staring at her. No, damning her. Yes, he was in handcuffs. Yes, he was listening to whatever Shipley was saying to him. But this silent conversation was all about him and her.

You scared yet, bitch?

Audrey couldn't seem to catch her breath. Her hand fisted around the strap of her bag. She couldn't seem to look away from the vile promise in his eyes, either.

And then she heard, "Turn around, Smith."

Her breath rushed out in a gasp of relief as Alex pushed through the gate and inserted himself between Audrey and the defense table. She hadn't noticed it when she'd seen him earlier, but he must be back on the clock because at some time during the day, he'd changed into his SWAT uniform—long-sleeved black shirt over a turtleneck, black pants tucked into black army-grade boots, his sidearm strapped to his muscular thigh. Even from this view, he looked as imposing and official as the night she'd first met him.

Demetrius licked his lips and smiled. "I'm just enjoying the scenery, officer. There aren't any pretty girls where I'm at right now."

Tension sparked off every corded muscle. "Shipley, corral your client, or I will."

Shipley said something that displeased his client, but the courtroom officers were already pulling Demetrius away from the table. Alex stood fast, blocking Audrey between the table and the railing until Demetrius had been removed and Shipley was packing up his briefcase.

Only then did he turn. "You okay?"

His hand came up, but quickly dropped to his side. She couldn't tell whether it was the protocol taboo of keeping his hands off the A.D.A. in court, or their prickly argument this morning about giving her time to think through her feelings that made him limit his concern to the dark expression in his eyes.

Audrey nodded, wondering at her own wistful response to the fact that he *hadn't* touched her. She tilted her chin and pretended her nerves weren't still rattling. "I must be making pretty good progress on my case for him to think he has to scare me back into my place like that."

"Do you think it'd cost me my badge if I punched him out for leering at you that way?"

Screw protocol. She reached over and grazed her fingers against his. He needed to take a step back from his gangbanger instincts, and she needed…she just needed to touch him. She needed that inexplicable anchor she felt whenever she connected with him in some way. It was just a simple brushing of fingertips, down low between them where only someone who was looking for the forbidden contact might see. But it was enough to regroup and feel grounded again. "Take the advice of an attorney, Alex. I'm okay. Just walk me to my car. I want to get to the police station and talk to Demetrius's friend Tyrell."

"Uncle Mac set the stage for you to wrap up this trial, didn't he?"

"Are you related to every cop at KCPD?"

"About half of them, it seems." With a nod to Trip, who quickly exited the back of the room, Alex pushed open the gate for her and followed her out of the near-empty courtroom. "He'll pick us up at the side entrance so you don't have to run the gauntlet of reporters today."

"I have to say something to them."

"No, you don't. Do you know how hard it is to spot a threat in a crowd like that?"

"They'll hound me all evening if I don't at least give them a statement."

He stopped her at the elevator and indicated to others that they go on so that she and Alex could ride down in a car alone. "Fine. Make a statement. But no questions. I'll alert Trip."

By the time she hit the chilly sunshine on the sidewalk in front of the courthouse, Audrey wished she'd taken Alex up on his offer to sneak her out the side entrance. *Gauntlet* was right. When she exited the glass doors, enough lights flashed to temporarily blind her. The assault of questions was equally unnerving. She barely got a look at the bundled-up onlookers and pro-test signs across the street in the park when the cameras and reporters swarmed around her. The salt that had been put down to melt the sleet and snow crunched beneath her boots as she took an instinctive step of retreat.

She bumped into Alex's hand at her back and was reminded she wasn't facing this alone. Raising her chin to a level of authority and control she didn't quite feel, she quieted them long enough to make her statement.

"The prosecution's case against Demetrius Smith is proceeding according to the strategy the district attorney's office has mapped out. We have strong circumstantial evidence and a time-line of events that shows—"

"But you can't get any witnesses to testify against him, can you?" someone shouted.

"Do you think Trace Vaughn's murder silenced any hope of getting someone to come forward?"

She felt Alex shift behind her. "Just a statement, Red."

Audrey cleared her throat and continued. "We have more expert testimony scheduled for tomorrow, including a representative from the drug enforcement task force to detail Mr. Smith's criminal record."

"He's going to get away with killing that little

boy, isn't he?" She turned to the other side to face the new accusation. "Cade Shipley says you can't prove murder."

"Mr. Shipley is welcome to say whatever he wants. Of course, he's going to come out in support of his client."

She recognized Steve Lassen pushing his way to the front of the crowd and braced herself before he ever spoke. "He's got you running scared, doesn't he, Miss Kline?"

Alex's arm tightened around her waist, pulling her forward. "We're done here."

You scared yet?

Audrey planted her feet and faced Lassen's chubby red nose. "I didn't appreciate your article in the paper this morning, Mr. Lassen. It'd be nice if you'd stick to the facts instead of sensationalizing a tragic event."

He had the audacity to smile. "Which tragic event would that be? That kid's murder—?"

"That 'kid' is Calvin Chambers."

"—yesterday's bombing? Or your father's heart attack this morning?"

"How did you…? How dare you!" Every blood cell in Audrey's body swelled with fury. "My personal life doesn't have a damn thing to do with your story."

"Audrey." Alex strong-armed his way through the crowd, dragging Audrey along with him, forcing her into a trot to keep up. "He's baiting you. Now isn't the time to let those emotions go."

But Steve Lassen and a barrage of questions dogged their every step out to the street.

"Is Rupert Kline still alive?"

"What hospital is he in?"

"Any time now, Trip," Alex muttered, pulling Audrey into his arms and spinning her away from the crowd.

"Have you received any more threats from Demetrius Smith's crew?" Lassen prodded.

"Don't answer that."

Audrey twisted against Alex's grip. How did Lassen know these details? Did he really think his tabloid tactics were going to get him a regular assignment back at a legitimate newspaper? Or was he privy to inside information?

"Do you think you're going to live to see the end of this trial?"

Audrey felt the unwanted hand on her arm, urging her to turn. She saw Lassen's camera flash to capture her open-mouthed shock.

"Get your hands off her!"

In a matter of milliseconds, Lassen's grip on her arm popped open and Alex was shoving the bastard's face down to the pavement. Tires screeched to a halt on the pavement behind her and Alex raised his fist.

"Alex!"

A woman screamed. Cameras flashed.

"Taylor!" Trip called out.

Audrey yanked on Alex's shirt. But he'd already frozen at the sharp command.

"You—cuff this guy." Trip Jones ran up beside them, ordering the reporters back, summoning the uniformed officers nearby. He closed his big hands over Audrey's shoulders and pulled her back. "Into the truck, ma'am. Let's go, Taylor."

Steve Lassen spat out blood and cursed Alex for breaking his camera as two officers locked his wrists behind him and pulled him up. Alex rolled to his feet, his shoulders still heaving with every steadying breath, his eyes never leaving the reporter who'd gotten to her.

"Book this guy on assault and confiscate that camera as potential evidence," Trip ordered.

"What about my rights?" Lassen argued.

"What about *her* rights?" Alex crept forward. "You think terrorizing her makes a good story?"

"So I was right. The Society Princess has received another threat." Lassen made a terrible mistake. He smiled.

"Alex!" Audrey dove out of the truck to stop him from attacking the loathsome reporter.

She grabbed on to his belt and tried to pull him away.

But Trip was there first, one big hand on Alex's shoulder, warning him back—the other hand pointed at Lassen's face. For a big man with a booming voice, Trip's hushed words sounded far more dangerous. "Let me tell you one thing, Lassen. I may be twice this guy's size, but I'm not the one you want to be pickin' a fight with. Now you go quietly with these officers, or I'll add resisting arrest to the assault charge and trespassing in a restricted area without your press credentials."

The two officers pulled Lassen away from the scene, but the washed-up reporter kept right on talking. "You know, one of these days I'll get my regular job back at the *Journal,* and I'll be writing such an exposé about police brutality and how the rich girls in this town get to call the shots and the poor jerks like me have to bow down to whatever you say. I'm going to change things. You wait and see."

"Rich girls?" Audrey released a breath she didn't know she'd been holding. "He blames me for him getting fired at the *Journal?*"

Lassen was locked inside a black-and-white cruiser before Trip released his hold on Alex. "He's an old drunk who can't keep a job, so he's trying to prolong his fifteen minutes of fame. Don't let him get to you."

Alex shoved his fingers through his hair, leaving a rumpled wake. "I let him get to Audrey."

"No, you kept him from hurting her, from exploiting her."

Finally, Alex took his eyes off Lassen and glanced up at Trip. "Semantics, big guy. Now's the time when you should be giving me the lecture about the rookie forgetting procedure and losing his cool."

"If somebody I cared about was being mobbed

like that...?" Trip thumbed over his shoulder. "Get in the truck."

As the crowd dispersed and the legitimate reporters got on their phones and in their cars to call in their stories, Audrey climbed up into the truck between the two men and they headed toward KCPD headquarters just a few blocks away.

Alex glanced over and touched the smudge of dirt Lassen had left on the sleeve of her coat. "The next time I give you grief about checking your emotions, tell me to shut up."

"He's not allowed to touch her, Taylor." Trip stopped at a light. He checked the intersection in every direction, even using the mirrors to see behind them. "You did your job."

Did Alex notice that Trip had refrained from using his "shrimp" nickname? Alex's friend was backing him up. Understanding.

"Yeah. Just doing my job. Maybe I haven't

outgrown my street background as much as I thought."

"Alex…" Audrey began. Maybe Alex didn't hear the distinction Trip had made. He fisted his hand in his lap, seething in uncharacteristic silence beside her. She reached over and curled her fingers around his hand. "I was scared back there. It felt so personal, like it didn't have anything to do with the trial."

He instantly opened his fist and turned his hand to match his palm to hers and lace their fingers together. "I wouldn't have let him hurt you."

She squeezed his hand, believing his promise, thanking him. "I was scared you were going to get yourself into trouble. But mostly I was scared by how much I wanted to see you punch his lights out." His dark eyes narrowed quizzically and she shrugged. "Not very highbrow or politically correct of me, is it? He knew Dad was in the hospital. He knew about the threats. He said 'rich girl.'" Her hand shook inside Alex's grip. "I've lost two friends, Val Gallagher and Gretchen Cosgrove, to somebody the police are calling the Rich Girl Killer."

Alex brushed a tendril of hair off her cheek and tucked it behind her ear. "Sweetheart, he was pushing your buttons, that's all."

"He didn't give a damn that I might be upset or afraid. I wanted you to hit him, to shut him up." She paused as Trip moved into traffic again, waiting for the implication to set in. "See what happens when I get emotional? I don't cry pretty, my face turns pink and I want to hit something. And here I thought I'd been raised to be a lady. Does that make me 'street,' too?"

Trip threw back his head and laughed. She felt the tension in Alex finally relax. He lifted her hand to his mouth and kissed her fingers. He was grinning. "Audrey Kline, you've got so much class running through your blood that you couldn't be 'street' if I tattooed it on your ass." He leaned over and kissed her mouth. "But you're learning. Now let's go convince some Bad Boys to turn on Big D."

Audrey latched on to his hand with both of hers and rested her cheek against his shoulder. Maybe, just maybe, she could learn to live with her heart wide open the way Alex Taylor did.

If nobody killed her first.

Chapter Nine

Promising that she wouldn't leave her office until Alex came to escort her to the courthouse after their lunchtime recess the following day, Audrey finally got her first private moment since that morning. Pulling her gaze from the well-formed back of Alex's uniform as he strode across to Dwight Powers's office to make a requested report on her safety, she darted around to the chair behind her desk and picked up her phone to call Clarice Darnell's number.

Her father answered on the first ring. "Yes, missy?"

"Daddy? Why didn't Clarice answer? Isn't she there?" She stood up as quickly as she'd sat down. "I thought the whole point of you staying at Clarice's was so someone could be with you around the clock. Mrs. Puente can take care of you during the day and I'll be home tonight if you want to move back to the house. And what about the protection detail? Are they there?"

Rupert Kline's warm chuckle sounded perfectly normal. "You sound like an old mother hen. A police cruiser is parked right across the street, keeping an eye on things. Clarice is fixing me a sandwich. I was sitting right by the phone and saw your number so I picked up. You don't have to call me every two hours to make sure that I'm all right."

Audrey took a calming breath, forcing herself to remember that her father was as much of an adult as she was. "Are you sure this is a good idea? The doctor said that you didn't suffer a full-fledged heart attack, but…" That didn't mean she wasn't worried about him running across a subsequent threat and succumbing to the real thing. Getting away from the house, from her, might be another benefit to staying with his new lady friend. "You sound tired."

"The nurses kept waking me up throughout the night, checking my pulse and who knows what else. I swear I don't know how anyone can rest up in a hospital. Frankly, I'm glad to be here."

"Is she taking good care of you? Making sure you rest?"

"She turned all her work over to her assistant, Jeffrey, and is devoting her entire day to me."

"And tonight?"

Her father was chuckling again. "Are you worried we're going to sleep in the same bed?"

"Dad!" Oh, Lord, she hadn't gone there yet. Clarice's offer to care for her father after his release from the hospital this morning was a generous gift, and should have eased some of

Audrey's concern. But she knew where *her* thoughts had been when Alex had tenderly held her through the night again. And she was no more ready to admit that her father might be falling in love when she was barely able to get her head around the idea that she herself was falling for someone she never would have imagined herself with.

"You still there, missy?"

"I'm here." Audrey pulled her thoughts back to the conversation. "I guess I'm just not used to sharing you with another woman."

"Don't worry, dear. We're not talking about anything permanent yet. And if we do get there, you know that no one writes a better prenup agreement than I do." His words took the edge of her concern. "You're still the number one woman in my book. How's the trial going?"

In other words, change the topic already. Rupert Kline was a successful man and certainly no fool. *Duly noted.* Although the lawyer in her still wanted to question Clarice Darnell's motives for being so attentive to her father, Audrey was beginning to understand how insulated and lonely they'd become since her mother's death. If her father was willing to embrace a new relationship, maybe she should support his decision—and consider doing the same with Alex.

Audrey cleared her throat, tucked a stray tendril of hair into the bun at her nape and answered. "Technical stuff this morning, mostly. Cade Shipley seemed to have an answer to rebut almost all of the expert witness testimony I presented."

"Shipley is more interested in headlines than in justice. Just keep your head about you—you'll get the job done." He cleared his throat, changing his tone. "Have there been any more threats since that newspaper? Do the police have any leads?"

"They're working on it. The lab didn't find

any usable prints on the paper, and a Detective Fensom talked to the paperboy—he said a black man paid him twenty dollars to deliver that paper instead of the *Journal*." Audrey hugged her arm across her waist to ease the tension gathering inside her. If her father hadn't heard about her run-in with Steve Lassen yesterday afternoon, she wasn't about to tell him. "Thank goodness the boy wasn't hurt. I don't know if I could handle any more collateral damage because of Demetrius Smith."

"So KCPD thinks one of Smith's gang sent the threat?"

"I suppose." She pressed her lips together to keep any mention of the Rich Girl Killer from accidentally popping out. Audrey was sure the threats were all trial-related, but now that Lassen had thrown the idea out there that Val's and Gretchen's murders—and the threats against her—might be the work of a serial killer who targeted wealthy women, she was having a hard time getting the possibility out of her head. But no way was she going to repeat that sensationalized suggestion to her father.

"Is Officer Taylor keeping you safe? I warned him to keep a close eye on you since I can't be there to do it myself. He's screening your mail? Your calls?"

Despite her quest for independence, she was a little bit glad that in some ways she would always be her daddy's little girl. The love she heard in his overprotective words gave her the strength she needed to summon a smile. "He has me on a short leash, Dad. I haven't been anywhere without Alex or someone on his team keeping me company."

"Good. If they're not doing their job, I'll put in a personal call to Police Commissioner Masterson."

"Daddy—" A firm knock at the door made Audrey's pulse race for a moment, but the anticipation quickly diffused when she saw a tall blond in a suit and tie instead of a uniformed cop with blue-black hair. "I have to go, Dad. Harper's here."

"Tell him hello."

"I will. I love you, Dad."

"Love you."

Harper Pierce invited himself into her office as she hung up the phone. "How's Rupert?" he asked.

Audrey tucked her phone into her attaché. "The doctor says he'll be just fine. The pacemaker did its job. He needs his rest, of course, for a few days."

"Glad to hear that." His smile transformed into something closer to a scowl. "So you're not taking my phone calls now?"

With a guilty start, Audrey punched the buttons on her phone and discovered five missed calls from his number. She apologized with a shrug. "I'm sorry, Harper. It's been crazy the past few days. With Dad. And I've been in court—"

"Were you in court last night? The night before that?"

"What?" So much for idle chitchat.

"We need to talk. I figured in person was the only way I could get your full attention and make you listen to reason." He thumbed over his shoulder. "I waited until your shadow disappeared into Dwight's office."

Not this conversation again. Pulling back the sleeve of her jacket, Audrey made a point of letting Harper see her checking her watch. "Can we schedule another time to catch up? Lunch this weekend, maybe. I know you were upset when you left the house the other night, and I want to clarify any misunderstanding between us, but I do have to be at the courthouse in thirty minutes. With the press and traffic—"

"This can't wait." He took another step inside and closed the door behind him. His face was lined with concern when he turned to face her. "I'm worried about you. I heard about the bomb. That crazy reporter at the courthouse. I saw the picture in the paper."

"No serious harm done." She tapped the fading bruise on her cheek. "I have a bodyguard, Harper. I'm taking precautions."

"I'm worried about your feelings as much as your safety."

"My feelings?"

"You're vulnerable right now, Audrey. God knows you're attractive and a catch that any man with an eye to his future would want."

Not the smoothest of compliments, but she already understood where this friendly warning was going and bristled beneath the silky fabric of her blouse.

"When you're under stress, when you're frightened, it's natural to turn to the people closest to you. I thought you'd have the sense to turn to someone you know you can trust."

"Like you?"

"Yes. You're pushing away the people you've known for years and leaning on a man you barely know."

Audrey looped the strap of her attaché over her shoulder and circled around her desk. "I'm not leaning on anyone. I stand on my own two feet."

Harper's subtle step to the side blocked her exit. His handsome face wore an apologetic expression—the hand on her arm was gently familiar. "You're getting defensive already. I can tell you think you care about Taylor."

Think? She'd been doing nothing but for the past forty-eight hours. "Thanks for caring, but my relationship with Alex is my business, not yours."

Harper's fingers tightened around her wrist. And there was nothing handsome about the accusation in his eyes. "You're screwing him, aren't you?"

Audrey tugged her arm from his grip. "I beg your pardon?"

"He's not good enough for you."

Audrey's chin shot up. "He's a better man than you are. He'd never talk to me like this, like I'm still some impulsive teenage girl who doesn't know her own mind. This isn't the kind of support I need from you right now."

"I checked him out. You know Taylor's adopted?"

"Yes."

"And his real dad is in prison?"

Audrey pushed him aside and reached for the doorknob. "I don't know you anymore. This conversation is over."

He pulled her hand off the knob and turned her around. "I thought you and I had something special, Aud."

"So did I. A friendship." Was that hurt? Confusion? Anger she read in his eyes? "You keep insulting Alex Taylor and my intelligence and I'm not so sure we have even that."

As quickly as he'd grabbed her, Harper let her go. His posture sagged as he retreated a step. "After all we've been through together, you'd pick him over me?"

In a heartbeat. That was her gut answering. But how much of what she was feeling for Alex was gratitude? The way he made her feel so protected? Or even an honest amount of lust? Tamping down those unresolved questions, she reached behind her and opened the door. "I've tried to give you some leeway because I expect you're still grieving over Gretchen, and maybe you think I can take her place in your life. I can't. I'm not interested in doing that. Now I have to get to court. My escort is waiting."

She knew by scent and heat—and the shift of Harper's contemptuous gaze—that Alex was there. Right behind her. Backing her up.

"Is there a problem?" Alex asked.

"No. I'd like to go now."

"Yes, ma'am."

Audrey grabbed her coat and, with Alex's arm around her waist—between her and the friend she no longer knew—left the office without looking back, giving her parting words a double meaning. "Goodbye, Harper."

AUDREY'S STOMACH GROWLED loudly enough for Alex to hear it across the cab of his truck. He turned on his headlights and drove out of the KCPD parking garage into the last hurrah of rush-hour traffic. "Hungry?"

"What was your first clue?" She leaned back against the headrest and closed her eyes. "I guess between the trial and Dad, interviewing gangbangers who are too terrified or too loyal to say anything against Demetrius, and that run-in with Harper, I forgot about eating."

He liked seeing her kick off her high-heeled boots and wiggle her toes. While he'd keep his opinion of that bullying snob Pierce to himself, he understood that she'd been dumbfounded by whatever they'd argued about, and was probably mourning the loss of the relationship they'd once shared. Her devotion to her father and her dedication to her work were admirable traits, but sometimes she got wound up so tight that he didn't think she knew how to relax or have fun.

"Can I take you to dinner?" he asked.

"Are you asking me out on a date, officer?"

"Well, you saw for yourself after court today that your dad and Ms. Darnell have settled in for an evening of popcorn and DVDs while the sarge keeps an eye on them." He checked his watch, hoping it wasn't too late and his idea wasn't too lame for a woman like Audrey. "It won't be Brennan's on the Plaza, but I could rustle up some chow."

Her giggle was a lovely sound in her throat. He hadn't heard it often enough. "I'm not as high-maintenance as you think, Taylor. As long as it involves a cup of hot tea, I'm in."

Good. Then he had a plan. Someplace intimate, away from any crowds, where the service was stellar and the food even better. He turned north toward the City Market and pulled out his phone to make a reservation. Another set of headlights turned north about half a block behind him, and while he always took note of his surroundings, he also realized that they weren't the only people heading home for dinner.

Audrey was dozing as they neared their destination. Three cars were still with him as he turned into the working-class neighborhood where the best food in Kansas City was located. The headlights from downtown were still there, two cars back. He was aware, but not alarmed yet.

He wasn't sure his choice of dining would meet with Audrey's approval, but he knew it was where he needed to go tonight. He'd followed her to bed last night like some kind of eager adolescent. And with her tucked up against him, she'd slept while he lay awake for most of the night, content to simply be close yet wanting to be inside her all at the same time. He'd lost track of the hours he lay there, breathing in her sweet jasmine scent and wondering if he was as low-rent as Pierce seemed to think, believing that a man like him and a woman like her could be together—*should* be together. After damn near impulsively confessing his love and watching her throw on her armor and deny her emotions yesterday, and then reverting to his beat-down-the-enemy tactics he'd used on Steve Lassen, he needed a good dose of grounding, of familiarity, to get his head screwed on straight. He couldn't do his job, he couldn't do right by Audrey if he couldn't get himself centered again. So yeah, this dinner was about what *he* needed.

Still, he'd better wake her up and give her a

chance to put on a little bit of that armor before they arrived. "We're almost there. Your father seemed to think you have a pretty good strategy lined up to take down Demetrius Smith."

"It is if we can keep Tyrell Sampson alive until he testifies."

"He's under protective custody with Holden and Trip watching over him. You can't get any safer than that."

She glanced over at him. "I might debate that."

Right. Like he hadn't blown his protection duty yesterday afternoon when he'd put the beat-down on Lassen. The majority of his SWAT training had taught him that the best security was about planning, controlling every possible variable and being aware of his surroundings— not violence after the fact. Although he'd been trained to carry out the necessary violence, it was supposed to be a last resort, not a gut reaction to some creep putting his hands on Audrey.

He vowed to do better by her next time. Alex

turned onto his grandparents' street. "Do you think Tyrell will stick to his word and say what you need him to up on the stand?"

She hummed as she stretched out her arms and legs. "He will if he doesn't want to go to prison for Calvin Chambers's murder. Because right now, all the evidence points to him as the shooter." She reached down to wedge her feet back into her boots. "Did you see how skinny he is?"

"Probably from the meth he uses."

"I'm half tempted to have Demetrius try on the jacket he claims is his as a visual aid for the jury. There's DNA from both Demetrius and Tyrell on both jackets. But no way does that medium-size hoodie fit him."

"Uncle Mac did say the zipper ripped."

"They had to have switched clothes after the shooting." She pulled down the visor in front of her, turned on the lighted mirror and combed her fingers through her hair. "And if that doesn't work, I guess I'll just have to get Big D to confess."

"If anybody can talk a man into confessing…"

"That better be a compliment."

They were both smiling when he pulled into a parking space at the curb.

"Taylor's Butcher Shop." She read the darkened sign over the closed shop. "Where's the restaurant?"

"Upstairs."

Now she got it. "Alex, I don't think I'm up to meeting your family tonight. I'm wrinkled and tired—"

"And they'll love you. It's just Grandma and Grandpa. They live over the shop. They're retired and he's leasing it to someone else—but I promise you, you can kick off your shoes when you're inside, and Grandma will have a cup of tea."

She thought about it for a moment, then smiled. "Okay. I want to meet this lady who taught you all those old-school manners and whipped you into shape."

"If you still have that bandanna on you, it'll make her cry." Audrey's face blanched. He saw her glance down to the attaché at her feet. His heart flip-flopped inside his chest. "Seriously?"

"I meant to take it to the cleaners. That's all. You know how busy we were today. I just didn't get it done." She reached for the door handle. "I'll leave it here."

"Hold on." He caught her wrist and stopped her from opening the door, keeping an eye on his side-view mirror.

"What is it?"

The car that had been following them all the way from downtown slowed down, but drove on past. Alex memorized the model and make of the sleek black car, but noted, "No license plate." He didn't like that. He released Audrey and pulled out his phone. "Give me a sec."

"Should I be worried?"

"I'm not sure. Yeah, this is Alex Taylor." He spoke into the phone, gave his ID number and reported the suspicious car. The car disappeared two corners down and Alex quickly got out and circled around to open the door for Audrey. He locked the door and tucked her under his arm, keeping his body between her and the street as he walked her through the door and up the stairs to his grandparents' apartment. "Thanks. Keep me posted." He clipped the phone back onto his belt. "They'll see if they can get a black-and-white to track it down. See if it's stolen. You didn't recognize it, did you?"

"To be honest, I wasn't looking. Do you think it's the Broadway Bad Boys?"

He wasn't convinced. The car might be stolen, which was definitely a trademark of the gang, but it was too nice a vehicle not to be stripped for parts yet, and it hadn't been souped up enough to meet the gang's need for speed and power. That left…? Hell, what did that leave—

something to do with Audrey's suspicion about a link to the Rich Girl murders? Like that was a better option for being followed than a bunch of gangbangers who wanted to frighten her into losing the trial?

"Let's just get inside." He knocked on the apartment door.

A moment later it opened to a robust, gray-haired man who still sported a military cut and posture despite the arthritic bend to his knees. "Come in, come in."

"Grandpa." He pulled Audrey inside and closed the door before trading a hug that included a couple slaps on the back.

"Alex." Their host extended one of his gnarled hands to Audrey. "I'm Sid Taylor, Alex's grandpa. Welcome to our home."

"I'm Audrey. Thank you, sir. It's a pleasure to meet you."

Martha Taylor came hurrying from the kitchen, wiping her hands on her apron before opening her arms wide. "And who is this handsome young man in uniform?" Alex traded kisses and a tight hug before she pulled away and beamed a beautiful smile at him. "Whenever I see you dressed in your work clothes, it makes me think of the first time I met your grandfather. He was in uniform, too. Such a handsome man." She cupped Alex's cheek before turning to Audrey. "Introduce me to your beautiful new friend."

Audrey extended her hand, her cheeks turning rosy with a blush. "Audrey Kline. Nice to meet you."

Martha clapped her hands together. "The famous lawyer from the newspapers. Well, this is an honor. Sid, you should have warned me. If I'd known we had a celebrity coming, I'd have fixed something besides leftover meat loaf." She arched one silvery-blond brow in apology. "But I do have a pie."

"What kind?" Audrey asked.

"Apple."

"Do you have a slice of cheddar cheese to go with it?"

"I think so."

"Oh, I am so going off my diet tonight. Hot tea and apple pie with cheese sounds like heaven to me."

Martha linked arms with Audrey and invited her into the kitchen. "It's a recipe I got from my mother. I get carried away with baking this time of year..."

Sid nodded his approval to Alex as they followed them in to dinner. "A woman with real class has class in any situation, even when she's served leftovers."

"I love Gran's meat loaf." Alex followed Martha's standing orders and stopped at the credenza outside the kitchen, removing his service weapon and setting it safely out of the way before sitting down at the table.

"So do I. That one's a real lady, son. Just like your grandma."

"You think I've got enough class to match up with that? For the long haul?"

His grandparents' home was more than a haven where Alex could relax for a couple hours. Sid understood that he'd come for a little friendly advice, too. He clasped his hand over Alex's shoulder. "The real question is, do you have enough love?"

"I've only known her for a few days. It's crazy how fast I thought I knew, but…I don't know."

"Could you stand to lose her?"

That took him aback. Alex looked up into Sid's eyes, eyes that were dark enough to make them look like blood relations. Maybe he should trust his instincts with Audrey. But could he convince her to trust hers? It was an all too important debate that he'd file away for later. "I'm hungry, Grandpa. Let's eat."

AUDREY WAS EMBARRASSINGLY full, totally exhausted yet curiously content after spending the evening with Alex and his grandparents. It made the trip home to an empty house seem a little less daunting, her father staying the night with his new lady friend a little less worrisome, and her feelings for Alex Taylor a little less frightening to admit.

To herself.

Alex had backpedaled a long way from his *We fit* and *I don't question it* lecture. Last night, although his actions had been tender, he'd been curiously quiet—and she'd been too exhausted to restart the debate. Maybe he'd begun to rethink his belief that some people could know each other, love each other—if they were the right two people—after a short period of time, just as she was beginning to consider it a real possibility.

He seemed to have a very special bond with his adoptive grandparents—and they clearly adored him—and seemed to have enjoyed their evening together. Martha Taylor had shared a lovely romantic story about meeting Sid for the first time, and how quickly she'd discovered that he was the man for her—for almost fifty years now.

But Alex had continued to be unusually quiet on the ride home. Not that he'd been rude—he'd answered every question she'd asked, and had cut short the phone call that told him KCPD had had no luck finding the car he suspected had been following them. Audrey stole a glance out the side-view mirror to see if she could spot any mysterious black car trailing after them as Alex swiped the key card and opened the front gates. He waited until the gates had locked securely behind them before turning his lights on high beam and following the long drive to the house.

When they cleared the trees and began to curve around the circle, Audrey was reminded of growing up here. "When I was little and we'd drive to the house at night—when the windows were dark like they are now—I always thought this big, stern facade looked like a multi-eyed monster's head." She pointed to the corner tower where her rooms were located. "I imagined the house was a creature with one horn, frozen in stone by some powerful wizard."

"That's a little fanciful for you, isn't it?" He said just enough to keep the conversation going. "It'd make a great Halloween house, though."

"Not that we ever had any trick-or-treaters." But despite the isolation, Audrey had plenty of good memories here. "I used to have parties here when I was a kid. We'd play hide-and-seek for hours. Charlotte had the best imagination—we'd find her up trees or in the root cellar or hiding between floors on the dumbwaiter. Harper—"

"—probably was more interested in winning than anything else."

"You do get to know people quickly, don't you? His favorite game was tag—mostly be-

cause he could outrun the rest of us. I wish…"
She paused with a heavy sigh that sounded like
pure sorrow. "I wish I'd seen that coming today.
Somehow his feelings for Gretchen must have
gotten all twisted up with what he used to feel
for me—back in high school. I haven't felt anything romantic toward him since then. It's not
his place to be so possessive or to assume any
kind of relationship. I made that clear, didn't I?"

"If you didn't, I will."

She was smiling again as he pulled the truck
to the bottom of the porch steps. "You can park
in the garage out back if you want."

He shook his head as he killed the engine.
"Too far away from the main house, and I know
the entrances and exits on this side of the house
better, in case we need to get out quickly."

Her amusement at his own possessive impulse
quickly vanished. "Are you expecting trouble?"

"I want to be prepared so that nothing catches
me by surprise." His smile tried to reassure her.

"It's just a precaution. With Holden and Trip babysitting Tyrell tonight, I don't have the same backup I did last night. Captain Cutler ordered some extra patrols to swing by the house. He said to call if I needed anything else. In the meantime, all you've got is me."

She reached across the seat to take his hand. "Then I'll be just fine."

Audrey reset the alarm system as soon as Alex bolted the front door behind them. She dropped off her attaché bag in her father's office, gave herself a moment to absorb his lingering presence, and really feel that he was going to be all right and back home in the morning. Then she peeled off her coat, kicked off her shoes and headed upstairs while Alex made a sweep of the house.

She was curled up in her peach silk pajamas, sitting on top of the flowered comforter in her bedroom, when she heard Alex enter the sitting room on the other side of the door. "The house is secure, Red," he called out. "Pleasant dreams."

But she couldn't get an answering "good-night" past her lips. As weary as she'd been after leaving the police station and Clarice's, their visit with his grandparents had revital-ized her. Her brain was running ninety miles a minute, going over everything she was feeling, thinking of the words she should say. Why had Alex's demeanor changed since that takedown of Steve Lassen at the courthouse? Had her ad-mission about wanting to clobber the guy herself shocked him? Changed his opinion of her? Had Sid or Martha said something that put him in this distant state? Or was he simply concerned about her security—so focused on that that he had no room for anything else in his head right now?

In the end, she took a page from Alex's own book. Quit overanalyzing everything. Don't muddy up her wants and needs with too many words. If she had a feeling about something— or someone—she should trust her gut and *do* something about it.

Audrey inhaled a steadying breath and slipped out of bed. Time to do.

She soundlessly opened the connecting door and found him hanging his Kevlar vest over his black uniform shirt on the back of a chair. He peeled off his black turtleneck with the white SWAT letters embroidered at the neck, and tossed it onto a stack of pillows at the end of the couch.

"Did you need something?"

His back was to her and she'd barely breathed, yet he knew she was there behind him. She took another step into the room. "Are you psychic?"

He glanced over his bare shoulder and grinned. "I smelled you. Jasmine or lilacs— some delicate perfume that clings to your hair."

The compliment danced along her skin and fluttered inside her. "Sounds like my shampoo."

The man was a poet in the most basic of ways. Her eyes were instantly drawn to the scar on the back of his shoulder. Whatever hard edges and insights into people he'd learned on the streets growing up, the Taylors had fine-tuned into something beautiful. Alex was the best of both worlds—smart and observant, tough, funny, caring and kind. And freaking hot when he moved around without a shirt like that.

Audrey cleared her throat, feeling the heat creeping up her neck as she tried not to notice every flex of muscle along his arms and back as he sat to untie his boots. "I think your grandmother may be a little psychic. Apple pie is my favorite dessert. Mom and I used to spend a lot of time in the kitchen—she went to culinary school and loved to cook. I've tried several times since she's been gone to make her pie, but I can't get the crust quite right. Martha said she'd share her recipe."

Alex dropped the second boot and pulled off

his socks. "That's like opening up the vault at Fort Knox. She must like you."

"I know. I'm practically a stranger. That's so generous of her. I think maybe she sensed that I was missing my mother—"

"You know, you're talking a whole hell of a lot for a woman I thought was coming in to say good-night." Alex stood and crossed the room to stand right in front of her.

She closed her eyes and trembled, savoring his gentle touch as he traced the pattern of heat coloring her neck and jaw.

"So what's this blush really saying?"

Audrey blinked her eyes open to the whisper of Alex's warm breath caressing her sensitive skin. His eyes were so close, so deep, so beautiful—his jaw needed a shave—and his lips... she couldn't seem to look away from his strong, supple mouth.

"Talk to me, Red."

She followed the movement of his lips and felt

something warm and wicked clench and release deep inside her.

"I wanted to say…" *Don't overthink this, Audrey. Do it.* She touched her fingertips to his stubbled jaw and lifted her gaze to his. "Are you sleeping in here tonight?" She walked her fingers to the nape of his neck and slid them up against the silky midnight of his hair. "I don't want you to."

His hands settled at the nip of her waist, branding her through the thin layers of silk. His nostrils flared as he inhaled a deep breath. "I may not be the gentleman you think I am, Red."

Just the words she needed to hear. Whatever was troubling Alex, it wasn't that he regretted admitting he had feelings for her.

She wound her free arm up behind his neck and retreated a step, pulling him with her through her bedroom door. "Maybe I don't want you to come in here and be a gentleman." His eyes never left hers as he dutifully followed.

"Maybe I want you to tell me some more of those wonderful stories about your family." She ran her palms along the column of his neck and out across his shoulders, then down the hard cords of his arms, setting her hands on fire with the friction created by every hill and hollow of warm, male skin she explored. She caught her breath on a stutter and reversed the path, pulling herself closer, breathing harder, wanting more, until she had her fingers lost in the silky curls on top of his head. "We could make some stories...of our own." She angled his face down toward hers, caught her breath as the pebbled tips of her breasts brushed across his chest. "Last night, together, and the night before...that was really spec—"

"Shut up, Red." Alex planted his mouth over hers, sliding his arms behind her waist and pulling her onto her toes, crushing her breasts against the wall of his chest as he plundered her mouth.

Audrey fisted her fingers in his hair and held on as her toes left the floor entirely and he walked her backward until her thighs hit the edge of the bed. His hands roamed at will over her back and buttocks, the silk offering little barrier to every calloused caress. Audrey was no longer aware of breathing as he buried his fingers in her hair to guide her mouth this way, and then another—plunging in, supping, seducing with each kiss. He groaned deep in his chest as Audrey mimicked his demands, pulling him impossibly closer and thrusting her tongue between his lips to taste the moist fiery heat that threatened to consume her. She grazed her lips along his jaw, delighting in the sandpapery abrasion against her feverish bruised mouth.

Alex opened his hot, wet mouth over the throbbing pulse at the base of her neck and she gasped. The graphic heat she knew colored her skin responded to his every touch, sending matching ribbons of heat deep beneath the surface, making her small breasts feel molten and heavy, and intensifying the aching weight building between her legs.

Audrey gasped against his skin when he flicked his thumb over the painful nub of one breast. "I don't really want to tell stories."

"I get the picture," he rasped against her ear. "You're sure about this?"

In answer, Audrey leaned back against the cradle of his arms. Her fingers were shaky, she couldn't quite catch her breath, but she knew her own mind.

She unhooked the first button of her pajama top, and then the second, and then Alex grabbed it by the hem and pulled it off over her head.

Audrey reclaimed his mouth and held on as he laid her on the bed and followed her down. His sure hands that handled guns and grandmothers and bad guys with equal ease made quick work of their remaining clothes. She bucked beneath him as he closed his mouth over an aching breast and suckled her into a mindless puddle of want and need.

"Oh, baby, it goes all the way down. You're so beautiful." Her telegraphic skin betrayed every bit of emotion and desire—he was tracing a line from her neck. "So beautiful." Over one breast. "So, so beautiful." Down her stomach to—

"Al…ex—I…I…" She couldn't catch her breath, couldn't find the words. She clawed at his shoulders, snatched at his hair, tugged his face back to hers and silently pleaded.

He looked down into her eyes and grinned. "It's okay, Red. You don't have to talk."

He entered her on one long stroke and Audrey flew apart in his arms. She buried her face against his shoulder and cried out in pleasure against his skin. Then she simply held on as he moved inside her, lifting her to another crest before they both tumbled over the precipice together.

Afterward, Alex pulled back the covers and

wrapped his arms and body around her, sealing her in warmth and contentment, sheltering her with whispered praises and quiet strength.

Audrey drifted off to sleep in his arms. He was right. She didn't need words for this. She didn't need more time to know.

She loved Alex Taylor.

Chapter Ten

There was something about waking with a woman's warm, beautiful breast pillowed against his side that made Alex reluctant to tune in to what his other senses were trying to tell him.

It was especially hard when that woman was Audrey Kline, the icy, overanalytical, career-focused heiress who turned out to be a passionate, uninhibited, uniquely adorable lover who'd charmed his grandparents, welcomed him into her bed and opened up her mind to the possibility that the two of them could work. A gangbanger from the streets romancing Rupert

Kline's only daughter wasn't a match that would make the society page of the *Journal,* but it was a match that he hoped Audrey would still want to pursue once the Smith trial was over.

She didn't make him feel as if he was just a bodyguard or a boy toy as that crass Harper Pierce had suggested. When she cuddled up in a ball beside him and snored softly against his chest, Alex felt as if she was his woman, as if they were equals. When she cried her eyes out or admitted she had a temper or rolled over in the middle of the night with a drowsy *Can we do that again?,* he felt as if they could truly communicate on a level that most couples— no matter what class they came from—rarely achieved.

He'd certainly never had a woman get so deep inside his head and heart before that his grandfather's words had made him shudder as if he'd already been robbed of his soul. *Could you stand to lose her?*

Alex dipped his head and pressed a kiss to the crown of Audrey's hair, fearing that if he hugged her as tightly as he wanted to at that moment, he'd frighten her awake.

Even with the thin strip of moonlight sneaking into her room between the drapes and blinds, he could admire the porcelain beauty of her body exposed above the covers that had caught at their waists. And he didn't need any light to still know the smell of her on his skin, the taste of her in his mouth, the sounds of her earthy cries of pleasure in his head.

She made him stop and think.

He made her stop and feel.

This was exactly where he was supposed to be. Right here beside Audrey.

The problem was convincing her that was still the case outside of this bedroom. He needed Audrey's skills in arguing to persuade her that not only was a future together with him an option, but that he believed it was the only option for the two of them to be happy and find the balance they needed.

There. He had heard something. Alex stilled his breathing and angled his ear toward the window. *Thup. Thup.* The muffled sounds jerked through his muscles, honing his senses, alerting him to the threat of danger in the distance. Metal on metal. Car doors closing.

He untangled his legs from Audrey's and slid out of bed. He pulled on his shorts and black pants and grabbed his weapon off the bedside table. He crept to the window without disturbing the drapes and lined up his eyes with the thin beam of moonlight, scouting the trees out front for movement while he tossed aside his holster and cocked a round into the gun's firing chamber.

The click-clack of sound, or his absence from the bed, elicited a murmur from Audrey. She was stirring. Waking, but not yet aware.

He heard another car door slam and swung

his eyes back outside. Damn those trees! He squinted, peering through the shadows. Was that movement down at the gate?

Son of a bitch. Alex snatched his phone off the bedside table and punched in a number. The battle had come to him. And there wasn't anything standing between the multiple attackers skulking through the darkness outside the gate and Audrey, snug in her bed, except for him, his gun and the survival instincts that had kept him alive on the streets and forged him into the cop—into the man—he'd become.

When Michael Cutler's clipped voice answered, Alex didn't apologize for waking him. "Captain. It's going down. Kline estate. I need backup. Now."

He didn't need to clarify or wait for a response before hanging up. The clock was ticking. On silent bare feet he went back to the bed and covered Audrey's mouth. Her eyes instantly popped open, wild and afraid. "Shh. It's me, Red."

She nodded her recognition and he released her. Her gaze darted down to the gun in his other hand. "What is it? What's wrong?"

She sat up and scooted off the edge of the bed as he returned to the window. "I need you to get dressed. As fast as you can. Shoes you can run in."

"Alex?" She darted to her closet and grabbed the first pair of jeans and T-shirt she could find.

"We've got company."

She shoved her bare feet into a pair of sneakers. "Should I call 9-1-1?"

"We'll need all the help we can get." He plucked his cell from his pocket and tossed it to her across the room. She caught it and flipped it open with one hand, punching in the numbers while she zipped up her jeans. A woman with no undies who could catch like a center fielder would have been mind-numbingly hot if he wasn't so caught up in trying to figure out... "What the hell?"

He counted one, two, three—four unknown perps running *away* from the front gates. They crossed through the light from a streetlamp and disappeared into the trees several yards beyond the great stone fence. Gallagher Security better be picking up all that movement and sending over a fleet of squad cars—

Alex jerked his head away and cursed at the flash of light that blinded him a split second before a concussive blast rent the air and rattled the windows. They were too far from the gate to sustain any damage up here, but that wasn't the point.

"What was that?" Audrey asked, crouching near the bed.

The explosion at the gate had triggered the alarms. He had to give Gallagher credit for putting on a show big enough to deter most intruders. Floodlights outside turned the shadowed trees into a daylit forest. Emergency lights flashed on and off in Audrey's bedroom and under the hallway door. A siren pulsed, shrieking its warning and forcing him to shout.

"Come with me!" He grabbed Audrey's wrist and ran into the sitting room while engines revved and tires squealed through the night outside. He pulled the Kevlar off the chair and slipped it over her head. "Strap this on."

She tried to pull the vest back up. "We're under attack! You can't face them without any protection. You don't even have any shoes on!"

He tugged it back down and fastened the first Velcro strap beneath her arm. "I'm not asking you, sweetheart. Put it on."

Thankfully, she batted his hand away and took over. Alex didn't waste any time. The one good thing about a gang fight was that he could always hear the enemy coming—even over the blare of the alarm. He could hear the two cars speeding across the bricks with their music blasting and their souped-up mufflers roaring like doomsday.

"Where are we going?"

Alex squinted against the flashing lights and ran as fast as Audrey could keep up. "Your father's study." Leading with his gun, he took the stairs two at a time and circled around at the bottom. "It's the one room in this house that has no windows. And only one door. I want you to go inside and lock it—"

"Aren't you coming?"

"—and get underneath the heaviest piece of furniture you can find."

"Alex!"

"Smith's Bad Boys are here." He couldn't wait for the cavalry. He needed to get out to his truck and try to reach his Benelli shotgun and spare cache of ammunition. "That means guns and lots of bullets flying."

She clung to his free hand with both of hers. "What about you?"

"This is my job, sweetheart." He pushed her

inside. *No, Grandpa, I couldn't stand to lose her.* "I love you. Lock it."

He pulled the door shut, said a prayer and ran outside to meet the enemy.

THE BULLET RIPPED THROUGH Alex's shoulder like a red hot poker as the first car spun out on the driveway's frozen slush and careened into an unbending oak. He had no time to do more than grunt at the searing pain as he flattened his back against the side of his truck and dropped the semiautomatic shotgun at his feet. The weapon would be useless to him now that the muscles on his left side were shocky with the wound and he'd be unable to steady his aim or control the recoil with one good arm.

But his second shot had taken out the driver and bought him a few seconds to expel the spent magazine from his Glock and reload the gun with the spare mag from his glove compartment. He sucked in a lungful of cold air, letting the winter dampness cool his body and clear his head. Fifteen bullets. Another car coming. One target down, two scrambling out of the wrecked car—he must have wounded another of Smith's Broadway Bad Boys when he'd returned fire on the approaching vehicle because he'd counted three passengers when he'd first spotted the back window going down and the semiautomatic coming out. And who knew how many more with how many weapons were zooming up the drive with one intent?

To take him out.

"KCPD!" Alex shouted. The bright security lights and patchwork shadows among the trees were wreaking havoc with his 20/20 vision. He couldn't make a clean shot. "You're firing on a police officer! Drop your weapons!"

"You can't take all of us!" one of them shouted, peppering the opposite side of his truck with another spray of bullets. Alex crouched down, cocked his weapon.

"You're dead!" another shouted. More bullets. Speeding car. "And then the bitch is dead, too!"

Like hell. Nobody was getting to Audrey as long as he was alive.

With the revving engine roaring in his ears, Alex swung around, bracing his arm between the open door and hood of his truck, and returned fire. Fifteen. Fourteen. Thirteen. One kid went down, grabbing his leg and rolling.

On foot, Alex was evenly matched, but the car racing toward him gave his attackers an advantage he couldn't hope to defeat on his own. Two more shots forced the last kid to the ground. Twelve. Eleven. Windows going down. Guns coming out.

Don't react. Think. Do your job, Taylor.

Where the hell was backup?

Alex shifted behind the door and emptied six shots into the speeding Impala. Ten. Nine. The windshield cracked. Eight. Seven. A tire went out and the driver slammed on the brakes. Six.

The windshield splintered. Five. The front-seat passenger dropped his gun to the bricks and jerked back inside the car.

Another shot pinged off the hood of the truck and he ducked back behind the door. "Come on!" he yelled to the fates, knowing the odds were shifting, and not necessarily in his favor.

He was up, aiming. Four. Three. Two. The kid on the ground wasn't getting up again.

A siren wailed in his ears, battling with the strident pulsation of the estate's security alarm. A car screeched its tires on the wet bricks, its engine bellowing like two massive storm systems charging closer and closer on a collision course. Two? Another vehicle was coming?

One bullet left. One freaking bullet.

He was outmanned. Outgunned. The kiss of death in any gang fight.

Alex glanced up at the mansion's front door. His heart was pouring out with every pulse beat of blood that throbbed from his shoulder. "Audrey…"

Bam! The thunderous crash jolted through Alex.

But he wasn't hurt. He hadn't been hit.

He pulled up behind the truck's door. "Hell, yeah!"

The cavalry had arrived.

Sergeant Delgado had rammed his big truck into the Impala's back fender and was shoving it across the bricks until the screeching friction of the Impala's tires ended with a crumpling smash against the porch's brick foundation. Even before the gang's car was wedged in tight, Trip Jones jumped out of the truck, his PSD rifle already aimed through the car's back window.

"Taylor!" Trip shouted. "Report!"

Until Trip and Rafe had the guns secured from the gangbangers inside the Impala, Alex stayed hunkered down behind the protection of his vehicle. "SWAT is in the building," he muttered to himself, almost light-headed with relief as he checked his weapon, verifying the last bullet. Inhaling a deep breath, he realized that the light-headedness might have something to do with all the blood dripping down his left arm.

"Taylor!"

Alex exhaled a cloudy breath into the chilled air and raised his voice. "I'm here. Ammo's about gone. I'm hit. But it's not bad. I'm not dying today, big guy."

"Better not, shrimp." Alex slowly straightened as he listened to Trip and Rafe shout orders to the perps inside the car. Two were already facedown in the slush with their hands cuffed behind their backs when Alex peeked through the windshield. Rafe had a third teen by the arm and was putting him down on the ground beside the others while Trip pulled the passenger Alex had wounded out of the front seat. It took a matter of seconds to trade a few curses, assess that the wound was superficial and put that one down on the ground, too.

Trip and Rafe exchanged nods before the sergeant called out. "Clear!" He pointed his gun over the four perps and motioned Trip over to Alex's position. "Check him out."

"Got it."

"How many targets do we need to account for?" Captain Cutler's voice buzzed over the radio inside Alex's truck. With the team on-site, providing backup, Alex finally ventured from his hiding place to see the captain marching one handcuffed perp out of the trees. He nodded toward Alex. "You're out of uniform, son."

"Yes, sir." They all were. Underneath their vests and gear, everyone was in off-duty clothes. But they'd all shown up. For him. For Audrey.

Alex was part of a team. He was part of *this* team.

"I made four perps in each car." Alex gritted

his teeth and grunted a curse as Trip probed his wound.

"And Miss Kline?"

"Inside."

"It's through and through." Trip pulled off a black glove and wrapped his hand around Alex's forearm, checking his clammy skin and halting him from mounting up the porch to get Audrey out of hiding. "What's your body temp, frosty?"

"Good enough that you don't need to baby me." He pulled away from Trip's first-aid efforts and headed for the front door of the Kline estate. His gun hung at his side from his good hand. "I need to make sure Audrey's okay."

"Wait a minute," Rafe warned, his grousing tone echoing over the radio and from just a few yards away. "Eight perps?" He pointed to the ground where Captain Cutler was placing the teenager he'd escorted from the woods. "We've got five here."

Holden Kincaid strode up with the strap of

his sniper rifle secured over his shoulder. In one smooth motion, he pulled it down into his hands, arming himself. "Driver and one on the ground are dead out in the trees. Didn't spot any other movement out there."

Alex's gut twisted into a knot. "There's another one."

Each man instantly positioned his gun in a defensive stance. While Rafe kept the prisoners under control, the captain, Holden and Trip faced away from the vehicles, securing a circle, scanning the grounds. Captain Cutler was on his radio, calling in a fugitive alert to the KCPD cars they could hear approaching in the distance.

But Alex's instincts—a gut-deep dread—was already pushing him up toward the front door.

"Alex?"

He halted in his tracks at Audrey's hushed greeting from the open doorway.

He read the threat in the stark pale cast of her

beautiful skin even before he saw the white-capped gangbanger walking through the front door behind her—with his gun boring into the base of her skull.

His old buddy Sly from the courthouse—the slick-talking twenty-something who'd denied exchanging any kind of message with Demetrius Smith—had Audrey in his grasp and a gun to her head. And the bastard thought he could bargain with Audrey's life. "Now you fine officers put your guns down and get the hell out of my way. I'm taking your truck and I'm driving out of here. Or she dies."

AUDREY SHIVERED WITH the chill that shook her from the inside out. But the cold steel pressed against her scalp didn't scare her half as much as seeing all the blood staining Alex's bare chest and arm. He was only a few yards away, just a couple of steps below the edge of the porch. But with the lights flashing and the alarm blaring and a frightened, angry man holding her in front of him like a shield, Audrey couldn't reach out. She couldn't run to Alex. She couldn't help.

He was bleeding, maybe dying. Because of her.

No. Because Demetrius Smith and his thugs didn't understand anything but power and intimidation. They didn't understand compassion. They didn't understand healthy communication. They didn't understand caring.

But she did. Because of Alex Taylor, she did. A thought blossomed inside her head, even as Sly urged her forward, daring the five armed warriors facing him to back away.

Alex was breathing hard, his deep, rhythmic breaths forming white clouds in the air. But nothing could hide the rage and pain that darkened his eyes, or the deadly stillness that held every exposed muscle of his body tense and rigid. "Don't do this, Sly. Let her go."

She flinched as Sly poked the gun against her

neck. "Shut up! I said put down your weapons. You—toss it in the bushes." When Alex didn't immediately comply, he jabbed her again. "Toss it!"

"I'm doing it." Alex tossed his gun into the hedge beside the steps. And though he motioned with his uninjured hand for the others to lay down their weapons at their feet, his eyes never left hers.

At the edges of her hearing, she heard Rafe Delgado mutter something like, "Don't even try it." A handcuffed man on the ground reconsidered his decision to get up.

This standoff wasn't going to end well. When the shooting had ended and she'd heard the crash, Audrey had climbed out from beneath the desk in her father's study and hurried out to see if Alex was dead. If her heart would be crushed. But she'd run into a desperate Sly instead. His crooked white cap so at odds with the deadly intent of this attack.

"Now back up!" Sly ordered.

Alex didn't budge.

"You're going to kill me, anyway," Audrey pointed out, knowing that if she made it to that truck, her life would be over as soon as Sly drove her away. She looked straight at Alex, letting her fear and anger and desperate effort to be understood register on her face. "Isn't that what you said inside, Sly? My head was the trophy that would secure your position as Big D's number one lieutenant?"

"Shut up." Her pushed her another step closer to Alex.

"You'll never get out of here alive, kid," Alex warned.

Sly wouldn't listen. "Give me your keys."

"Well…you weren't nearly so eloquent, but I got the message. Kill me and Big D walks. And you'll have earned his everlasting gratitude."

"Red…"

Alex's gaze darted to Sly and the gun and

back to her before she continued. "I talked to Gallagher Security Services while I was hiding. I hear the sirens now. I asked them to send several ambulances—and all the backup they could spare. But I don't need any more backup, do I? You can take him out, can't you?"

"I'll kill you first, bitch."

Alex's dark eyes narrowed.

Understand me, sweetheart. Please understand. "You know, it's not politically correct, but...I'd really love to see someone put Smith and his Bad Boys in their place."

"Shut up."

Captain Cutler took a step forward. "Son, this is going to end badly for you. Put down your gun. There are five of us."

"And one of her." Audrey grimaced as the gun ground into her scalp. "Now back up." Alex's commander retreated a step as Sly turned his focus back to the more immediate threat. "Give me your damn keys or I'll do her right in front of you."

"Alex?" Audrey heard the spooky calm in her own voice and braced herself. "Give him the keys."

ALEX NODDED, HATING WHAT she was asking of him—and loving Audrey Kline for being smart enough, brave enough and trusting enough to ask it.

Could you stand to lose her?

He reached into his pocket for his key ring. "My grandpa says a class act is a class act in any situation. You're all class, Red."

"What?" Sly frowned. The bastard didn't know it yet, but he was doomed.

"Take my keys."

Alex tossed them. In the split second it took for Sly to release his grip on Audrey to catch them was all the time it took for Alex to attack. He charged up the stairs, lowered his shoulder and rammed Sly in the gut, taking him down to the porch as Audrey jumped to the side. Sly kicked. He punched. Alex grabbed at the wrist that held the gun, and managed to hold on, cursing as the kid rolled over on his wounded shoulder.

But Alex was too fired up to really comprehend the pain. This sicko had threatened Audrey, maybe hurt her, frightened her. Two people were dead in her front yard because this jackass thought he had the right to take down the woman he loved. No way. No. Freaking. Way.

With a surge of pure adrenaline to fuel his strength, Alex called on every fighting skill he'd ever learned—on the street and at the police academy. In a matter of seconds, he had the advantage. He was on top. Sly was unarmed. And when he tried to rise up to hit Alex's wounded shoulder, Alex finished it.

One punch. Down and out. The white cap went flying and Sly collapsed onto the porch, his eyes woozy, the fight knocked right out of him.

Spent, chilled, breathing heavy, feeling every ache of the past few minutes, Alex pushed himself up to his hands and knees and then wearily rolled to his feet. He turned, stumbled forward—seeking one face, one reassurance.

Holden and Captain Cutler had Audrey secured behind them, but she was already pushing her way through. Trip was kneeling beside Sly and rolling him onto his stomach so he could put handcuffs on him.

Alex held out his right arm and pulled Audrey as tight against him as he could hold her. Her arms anchored themselves behind his waist as he pressed a kiss to her temple and whispered against her ear. "You're right, Red. That did feel good."

THE POLICE CARS AND ambulances were wheeling through the gates as the men of SWAT Team One finished securing the scene.

Alex was trying to brush the hair off Audrey's

face, find her mouth, find out if she was okay. "I'm so sorry. I didn't want this to happen this way. I told you to stay in that room. You're not supposed to be in the middle of my—"

"Your world?" She pulled Alex down to the step beside her and reached into her pocket.

Ah, hell. Either the shock from getting shot was wearing off, or he was getting sentimental himself, but he was grinning like an idiot when she pulled out *his* bandanna and pressed it against his wound. He jerked at the stabbing pressure, but his eyes never blinked, never wavered from hers.

"This is my world, too, Alex. But we're going to make it better. Together—we can make it better."

She leaned over and kissed him gently on the mouth. He moved his lips against hers and she kissed him again.

"You earned your keep this time, shrimp," Trip intervened, pausing as he walked Sly down to the driveway to razz Alex one last time. "You think he's one of us now?"

Rafe Delgado joined in. "Let's see. He took out five perps before we got here and he's got a bullet hole in him—I think he's passed initiation."

"Welcome to the team, Taylor." Trip made some sort of snorting noise that Alex barely heard as he leaned in to kiss Audrey again. "Oh, now he's gonna go and spoil the moment by getting all mushy with his girl."

Alex tunneled his fingers into Audrey's hair, touching her, verifying with his own hand that she was alive and safe. And his. "Damn straight."

Chapter Eleven

Messy. Messy. Messy.

He pounded on his steering wheel with both fists, wailing his fury against the black steering wheel until his fingers went numb.

How could Smith's men be so stupid? He had everything under control, everything in place to get Demetrius released after serving just a few months on a minor drug charge. Audrey Kline would have looked like a fool trying to pin that kid's murder on him. Like a pitiful, pretty little girl playing grown-up in a courtroom she could never hope to command. She wouldn't be able to save her own skin, much less the world if they'd let him destroy her the way he'd wanted.

He killed Trace Vaughn for them. After following Audrey and her bodyguard boyfriend from the Fourth Precinct station to that drab neighborhood where shopkeepers sold groceries and souvenirs to other working-class clods, he'd prepped an explosive for Tyrell Sampson's car. Yes, he was under police protection, but he'd be released after testifying. And all Demetrius had asked him for this time was retribution. Kill any Triple B who betrayed him, scare the others back into line so that they'd carry out his wishes even if he went to prison.

But tonight those idiot Bad Boys had taken the bomb and used it to go after Audrey themselves.

Idiots. Idiots. Idiots.

He spied the pack of cigarettes lying on the seat beside him and picked it up, tapping it on his hand three times and pulling one out. As he slipped the filter between his lips, he noticed one cigarette still sticking out of the pack. He pushed it down, taking an easier breath once the symmetry of the rectangular package had returned.

But it was only one easy breath. He felt the agitation growing inside him again as he watched from the shadows of his parking space. He lit his cigarette and counted the parade of police cars and the coroner's van driving in and out of the Kline estate. He didn't care how many Bad Boys were dead, how many went out in ambulances. He didn't care if the cops rounded up the ones who got away.

What he cared about was that Audrey could have gotten hurt. She could have been killed in that blitz attack.

And it wasn't their place to kill her. That was supposed to be his prize.

He inhaled a deep drag off the cigarette and tried to think. He wasn't done toying with Audrey, but the police would be all over her now—not just that pint-size cop and his SWAT buddies. It would be harder to get the messages to her. Harder to be there to watch her suffer. It would be damn near impossible for her to lose that trial now—if nothing else, after such a blatant, violent attempt on her life, she'd win the jury's sympathy vote. And the press's.

He took another hit off the cigarette. He could see it now—she'd be in all the papers again, but this time as a hero.

All he'd asked for was a little patience, the opportunity to carry out the plan in his way. But Demetrius's buffoons had ruined everything. He needed to end his ill-advised alliance with the Broadway Bad Boys and come up with a new plan.

Yes, that was it.

Audrey Kline wasn't the only woman who'd lied to him. Who'd led him on. Who'd wronged him. Let her have her moment of glory. There were easier targets who could give him just as much satisfaction. Maybe even more.

He knew countless ways to make his enemies suffer.

He pulled out the ashtray, snuffed out his cigarette and smiled.

He'd move on to the next victim.

AUDREY SAW THE BEADS OF perspiration dotting Demetrius Smith's upper lip and squelched the urge to smile. She set down her notes, took a deep breath and strolled back to the witness stand.

"So you admit that Tyrell Sampson was telling the truth."

"I told that fool to change jackets with me and keep his mouth shut. And then none of us would get taken in." Demetrius smacked his hand against his thigh. "But I only shot that kid in the leg. The most you can get me for is assault. Tyrell's the one who put that bullet in his chest."

"Your Honor…" Cade Shipley rose to his feet, slowly buttoning his suit coat, acting as if he wasn't worried that his client was destroying the defense he'd so carefully put together. "My client is charged with murder. That's the crime Miss Kline should be trying. All she's doing with this line of questioning is confusing the jury as to the legalities—"

"Is there an objection in there somewhere, Mr. Shipley, or are you just making a speech?" Judge Shanks groused. "I didn't think so. Miss Kline, continue."

"Thank you, Your Honor." She turned to Demetrius once more. "So you admit to shooting Calvin Chambers in the leg?"

"Tyrell said there were a couple of Warriors running through my yard, spying on us. In *my* territory. We shot a couple of times into the air to scare 'em off."

"But you didn't hit the two Westside Warriors on the scene."

"No, they were already gone. I didn't know that kid was there."

"The one you shot in the leg."

"Demetrius!" Shipley warned.

"What? I said it. I shot him in the leg." He scowled at Audrey. "Book me on that, sister."

Audrey smiled right back. "Your Honor, may we approach?"

Judge Shanks waved Cade and Audrey to his bench.

"Your Honor," Cade began, "opposing counsel is badgering my client."

The judge shushed him and pointed at Audrey. "She gets to talk right now. Miss Kline?"

"Your Honor, I just wanted to give Mr. Shipley a heads-up. If you recall the details of the medical examiner's report, Calvin Chambers was wounded in the chest. But that wasn't the kill shot. He bled to death—from a gunshot wound to his femoral artery." She turned to Cade. "Your client just confessed to murder."

ALEX WAITED A HALF HOUR for Audrey to accept her last handshake and for the courtroom to clear before he stood up from his seat in the back. "Congratulations, counselor."

"I won."

"That's right, Red. You did it."

"I won." Her cheeks bloomed a bright pink as she shook off her staid, proper, public demeanor and shot her arms up into the air. "I won!"

Reveling in her emotions, fists pumping, she ran through the gate, straight down the aisle and leaped into Alex's chest, hugging him tight around the neck as he swung her around. It wasn't the easiest thing to hold on to her with his left arm tied up in a sling, but he'd damn well do whatever he had to to keep this woman close to him. Forever.

"I have to call Dad at his office and tell him the good news. I think he'll be proud of me. I'm proud of me."

"Add me to the list, too." When his shoulder

started to ache, he set her down, but he couldn't let her go. He brushed aside the auburn tendril that had fallen across her cheek and pressed his lips to the warm spot there. "I bet if you come with me to the Shamrock Bar tonight, you'll find a whole room full of cops who'll want to shake your hand and buy you a drink. I know of at least five SWAT cops who'd like to drink a toast to you for getting Demetrius Smith off the streets and pretty much decimating what's left of one of the most dangerous gangs in town."

"I couldn't have done it without you, Alex. And the rest of SWAT Team One."

Yeah. He owed a lot to Trip, Rafe, Holden and Captain Cutler.

"Not just to keep me alive or to keep the press at bay or to keep my father from worrying himself sick about me—but I needed you to believe in me. I needed you to help me understand that I could do this."

"I never had any doubts."

"Yes, you did."

"Audrey." So she'd proved him wrong. She'd shown him that first impressions weren't always the right impression. And he'd be forever grateful for that lesson. He leaned in to kiss her. "You're right. Point taken."

"Wait." She pressed her fingers against his lips and pushed him away. "I'm not done talking."

"I conceded the argument. You're sure you don't want me to kiss you?"

"Alex." Her fingers trembled against his mouth with a gentle, tempting caress.

She was probably remembering where the last few kisses between them had led, and the courtroom probably wasn't the best place for *that* kind of interpersonal communication. With a reluctant sigh, he pulled her hand down and laced their fingers together to walk her to the front of the courtroom and collect her things.

"Come on. We can continue this discussion at home. Trip's waiting outside to drive us. If the Rich Girl Killer had anything to do with this nightmare, I'm not taking any chances. I asked the guys to help me keep an eye on you until I'm back at a hundred percent."

She pulled her hand from his. Planted her feet. "No. I mean, yes, that's really generous of them and I can never thank them enough for all they've done. But I have something private to say that can't wait any longer."

She tilted her chin to that vulnerable angle that had first tempted him to take her in his arms. But he listened. Audrey Kline had something to say, so he listened.

"I love you. Just in case it isn't perfectly clear. Just in case you think you're the only one who can say it or I don't know how to say it or I'm afraid to say it—I just want you to know that I love you, Alex Taylor."

He smiled. "Trip can wait. Now can I kiss you?"

She smiled. She wound her arms around his neck and pulled his mouth down to hers. "I'm done talking. It's time to do."

* * * * *

Mills & Boon® Online

Discover more romance at
www.millsandboon.co.uk

- **FREE** online reads
- **Books** up to one month before shops
- **Browse our books** before you buy

...and much more!

For exclusive competitions and instant updates:

 Like us on **facebook.com/romancehq**

Follow us on **twitter.com/millsandboonuk**

Join us on **community.millsandboon.co.uk**

Visit us Online   Sign up for our FREE eNewsletter at
www.millsandboon.co.uk